An Attem

Exhausting a Place in

Leicester

Edited by Jon Wilkins

Cover and all illustrations courtesy Sarah Kirby

www.sarahkirby.co.uk

An Attempt at Exhausting a Place in Leicester

Jon Wilkins

Visit my website at www.jonathanwilkins.co.uk

ISBN: 978-0-244-47534-5

JON WILKINS

Writer, husband and father to two young men, Jonathan lives in a small village in Leicestershire, with his beautiful wife Annie.

Acknowledgements

With grateful thanks to Russ Murchie, Stephen Booth, Clare Hardy, Michael Darmian, Gary Nelson, Joss Wilkins, Nick Nenadich, Jim Maguire, David Gill, Foqia Hayee, Pam Thompson, Alun Robert, Emma Lee, Nicola Humphreys, Nicola Allen, Laure Roux, Nicola Koncarevic, Tom Conway, Mark Newman, Jenny Drury, Muir Sperrings, Julie Gardner and Alexa Fears

To Annie my darling wife.
My two wonderful sons David and Charlie.
To my brother Joss.
To Viv and my Parents, who I miss terribly.

Contents

Foreword

I was relaxing at my work desk reading my favourite Francophile crime writer, Cara Blacks "Murder in Saint Germain". Her hero, Aimée Leduc scoots around Paris solving crimes. Paris is the key, the second most important character in her books. Aimée's partner, Rene, mentions Georges Perec and his writing in the story.

This seemed interesting so I looked further and found that in 1973 Perec spent three days in St Sulphice, Paris, just watching Paris and its people which resulted in a creative wonder that is "An Attempt at Exhausting a Place in Paris".

Inspired by Perec's work, I thought is it possible as a writer to exhaust a place. Could you possibly wring out everything about a city so that there was nothing left to write?

To me that is an impossibility and by looking through the submissions in this book I think you will agree. For every work accepted, two or three were rejected, as there was simply no more room for them.

It was heart breaking to have to turn down so many writers. But on the positive side, there are SO MANY writers out there which is wonderful.

You cannot exhaust a place with words. There are so many words and in the most part they are words unspoken so this was a chance for people to speak and to put words onto paper and to present them to the reader.

This sounds quite straight forward but isn't remotely. But what has been amazing is the diversity of talent that has been uncovered through these submissions. Beginners and veteran writers, poets and prose writers as well as some non-fiction. I have been so pleased with the pieces I received.

Variety is indeed the spice of life and there is as we say an infinite variety here. Places from all over the city and county are described from all ages, Vikings, The War of the Roses, of course and so many nostalgic pieces that go to the very heart of the book.

What is a piece of writing if it is not set at the heart of the topic written about? I asked for pieces to be written with love of Leicester, a passion for Leicester and have been grandly rewarded. The pieces all get to the heart of Leicester and it is a vibrant beating heart at that!

As Editor I have tried not to change too much as I am aware how writers take ownership of their work and find it hard to let go. But we also have to be aware that once the words are released into the world, it is for the reader to see what they mean and to interpret them as they see fit. The end result might be dramatically different from what the writer initially meant, and it is that reinterpretation that is the beauty of writing and reading.

What I can be sure about is that each writer has a love for Leicester and has shown it through their work. That was the most pleasing thing for me.

Please enjoy this anthology and then please write about Leicester yourself. Tell the tales of the city and the county that you know about. Or make something up. We should all write as often as we can and writing about a place you love is the best place to start.

Jon Wilkins
Editor

MARK NEWMAN

Has been shortlisted for the Costa Short Story Award, highly commended in the New Writer Prose & Poetry Awards and Bristol Prize longlisted. His debut short story collection My Fence is Electric and Other Stories will be published by Odyssey Books in February 2020.

MORE THAN JUST A CHEESE

And I stepped off the train and onto the platform - my first footfall in Leicester. I had on red jeans like the ones River Phoenix wore in My Own Private Idaho so you could recognise me. I stood on the platform and the train pulled away. A billboard was revealed - "Leicester - more than just a cheese". I bloody hope so, I thought. I waited there; my Leicester was so small then, just the platform, no knowledge of what lay beyond. It felt as if I was underground with the coverings above my head. I had nowhere to go if you didn't meet me. I wondered where you were. Now you would text me and say, "where are you" and I'd say, "on the platform" and you'd say, "I'm in the foyer, upstairs" and you'd add a rolling eyes emoticon, or that one where the head is on its side and laughing and tears stream from its eyes. We'd written letters to each other for months, some only two or three days apart. I still have them all. Do you?

I met a boy from Nottingham at the station foyer a few months later, standing in the same spot as you waited for me. We went to the Dover and he dropped his cigarette in his beer and talked to my crotch the whole time. I took him straight back to the station foyer and he said, "am I going back then?" and I said "yes" and turned and walked away, a bravado born from anger at the path his eyes took when he spoke to me.

The station looks the same, doesn't it? I don't think anything's changed, has it? If we stood there again, we'd be the same, but older.

We got a taxi to your house, I think. Perhaps I glanced up at the YMCA as we passed? It's an impressive looking building, I'm sure I would have noticed it. Two weeks later I was living there - Room 315, windowsill so wide I could sit on it and read - I watched the Caribbean Carnival go by that first year I was there. I stared up at the tower block opposite, the shadows in the windows. I ate Findus Crispy Pancakes, peas and white bread and watched Absolutely Fabulous and Tales of the City. For a while I was on the cover of the leaflet in the foyer and on the back of it a picture of the room opposite mine, decorated with my Marilyn Monroe poster and one of my shirts draped on a chair. I remember an Italian boy lived in a room along the corridor and would walk to the shower with a small towel around his waist. Outside the YMCA there was still the subway to get across to the station and I used to give my last change to the guys who slept under there at night.

We must have got a taxi as I would have had bags, but in my memory, we walk along the canal. I'm sure we did that at some point in the fortnight I stayed at your house. I walked that route last week - it has changed so much in places. The area opposite Castle Park was building land when I moved here, I think, with wooden fences, eight-foot-high, and a walkway between that zig-zagged sharply so you were never sure who was coming towards you. Why would I have been walking across there? I can't think now. The canal pathways were lined with thick hedges and here and there the homeless were living, sleeping bags unrolled; every now and then I would hear a rustle and be surprised by a face looking back at me. Now, in places, the hedges have been thinned, or cleared. There are benches, picnic tables. There are houses and supermarkets. There are roads. Across the canal the football stadium looms. The weir and the birds and the quiet. The weir and the birds and the pitch and the fall of the crowd. They tore Braunstone Gate Bridge down, do you remember? And I didn't join a march or campaign or write a letter or set ink on a placard, but I watched it all happen with sadness. You could walk along the old railway line for miles and end up at that bridge, but I can't remember where it started off or how you got there.

We talked tennis - Wimbledon had just finished, hadn't it? And music. I talked about history and you talked about art. In the weeks that followed I looked for the history in the city, staring at a castle in the distance then, getting closer, finding it to be the prison. The castle, when I did find it, was nothing but a pile of rocks on the ground. Castle Park – a park with no castle. But there was a king in a car park, all that time, patiently waiting for his moment to come. He's buried now under a chunky slab in the cathedral. And how disappointing was the cathedral to me, coming as I did from Ely? I have grown to love it over the years - I like the way they light it at night, I get pleasure from the jaunty angles of the chairs outside. I proposed to my husband there, long before we were allowed to be married, at a Vivaldi Four Seasons concert by candlelight, I leaned across and whispered, "Will you marry me?" and he smiled and said "Yes".

Once you'd shown me the canals, I walked them for miles in each direction. There was a day I walked for hours until my feet blistered, and I trudged away from the water at the first sign of a road thinking I would get a bus into town, wondering how far out from the city I was, only to find I was in Wigston. I carried on walking and was home within the hour.

We dropped my bags at your house, and you took me for a walk around the estate and sat in the park. You told me about the parks in Leicester and later I walked through Abbey Park. Always one to scurry out of sight at the first opportunity I took the Nature Trail and every few yards there was a man nodding and smiling and saying hello and I thought, how polite Leicester people are, how charming. I looked for the Abbey, and when I found it there was nothing but a pile of rocks, and not even the original rocks. Abbey Park – a park without an abbey. I joined the canal here too, walking past old warehouses, whose smashed windows suggested desolation but there were sounds of machinery from within. Are they still there, or are they now luxury flats? I haven't walked that way for years. Later, the ground parted and the Space Centre rose up and took its place.

Victoria Park, too - I weaved my way across it following nights at Streetlife, thinking how beautiful it was lit up on all four sides, the Memorial, De Montfort Hall and the trees. I went to the Radio 1 Roadshow there and have to check Google to confirm that I saw the people I thought I saw – Coldplay, Faithless and Kylie Minogue. The date: September 2, 2001. I saw Moulin Rouge at the Odeon Cinema while the towers were falling and walked home elated by the joyous film and into my house where the TV was on.

But that was long after I arrived. I remember you talked to me about Streetlife and said you would take me, but I had been there already by the time we went together. I had put an advert in Boyz and been out with several men. One took me for a drink then offered to take me to Streetlife - "it's full of these dumb young bunnies who spend the whole night dancing" he said. You can imagine what happened when we got there and the music pounded its way into my head and I'd had something to drink, dumb young bunny that I was. One man lived in a converted church on South Albion Street. He bought me a drink and asked me if I liked opera. "No," I said. "Classical music?" "No," I said. He asked me what music I liked, and I told him. He looked at his watch and said he had another appointment and left me there alone, as if my musical taste was all that defined me.

I went alone to Streetlife quite often, did you know? I would eat pizza or curry in my flat, down a bottle of wine, throw up in my bathroom and head down there for 11pm, get onto the dancefloor and jump around until 2am, then go home. A man once gave me Poppers to smell and I put them to my nose and sniffed as I had seen other people do. "You have to take the lid off" he said when I handed them back. When the lights came on in the early hours you realised you were dancing in a warehouse, that the floors were littered and sticky, the walls just brick walls. There was The Pineapple, with its stripper nights, those oil-slicked dancers that did nothing for me. The Dover had blacked-out windows and you looked left and right before you went in – now, the rainbow flag flies and you can see in through the windows. I went there too without you, took the drinks that were offered and went home alone.

You took me to the cinemas and a few years later I worked in them, do you remember? -first the Odeon (now, when I go to the Curve I look across at the Athena and remember hanging the letters up at the front and slipping the posters into the display cases outside) and then the Cannon on Belgrave Street, with my white and blue stripy waistcoat which I only threw away recently. A group of us would trek round after work to Mr Yummy's around the back of Abbey Street, have Chilli Beer, when it was a new thing to have, and stay there until morning. Or I'd walk back to my then flat in Highfields past the prostitutes, who always said hello, and once a man stopped the car next to me and said, "how much? - I have jay cloths" and I had no idea how to respond. The fish & chip shop near my Highfields flat was glorious.

They tore the cinema down, but it is still built in my mind – the giant cinema screens, the red, red carpets, the staff endlessly dipping their hands into the popcorn, the winding staircases down to the exits.
I used to go to the Phoenix too, with Irish Michael – did you ever meet him? Did I introduce you? We would cross the road after, drink in the Magazine, and chat about the films we had seen. We once saw Ladybird, Ladybird and were so shell-shocked afterwards that we stood out the front of the cinema like we had lost our minds. "Shall we go for a drink?" I said. "I think I'll go home," he said. "Yes," I said. "Me too." He moved to America. He sent me a photo of him at a drag club, but I never heard from him again.

While I stayed with you, I went into the housing office which was at the top of Welford Road (I think the building is now a Tesco's). I said I needed somewhere to live so I could apply for a job in the city and they said I needed a job before I could apply for somewhere to live or was it that I needed somewhere to live before I could sign on and they said I needed to sign on before I could get somewhere to live? The man at the counter next to me said try the YMCA, and just like that I rooted myself in this city – by entering that building at a time that allowed me to reach the counter to be overheard by the man stood next to me. Sending out roots, growing up and out into this city - this city where I was told I would not belong until I had lived here twenty-five years and thinking, that's it then, I'll never belong, but last year it rolled around, that 25th anniversary date and I poured myself a glass of wine and raised it up and thought of how I met you that day on the station foyer and how Leicester had proved to be so much more than just a cheese. (But it's a good cheese - perfect for Welsh Rarebit and for the topping on a cheese and potato pie).

Did you ever go to Blackthorn Bookshop, on the High Street not far from Café Bruxelles? (Do you remember when that was the only café bar, then Fat Cat opened and we were all "ooh, two café bars in Leicester, how continental?"). Upstairs at Blackthorns was a gay & lesbian section (the other three letters not yet tagged on) and I could get my free weekly copy of Boyz (was it weekly? fortnightly?), and I would move away from that section if anyone came upstairs. When I left the shop my copy of Boyz was rolled tightly shut so no-one could see. Now boys (Boyz!) walk down the street hand-in-hand and it's wonderful to see - do you walk that way with your husband?

That first night I stayed with you. We stayed up late watching badly dubbed Japanese films that seemed to be on one after the other and we added our own soundtrack to the film's, cackling with laughter. You sat next to me in your boxer shorts and I thought it was all so risqué.

And then I was in your brother's bedroom and the door closed behind me and I looked out over the field (or was it fields?) behind the house and I did a little jig and I was so, so happy. Do your parents still live in that house? Are there still fields to see?

I haven't written you a letter in such a long time.

HELEN FRANCIS

Lives in Melton Mowbray, Leicestershire. Graduate of Brooksby Melton College and The Oxford School of Drama. Recently a Member of Liars League Leicester where she has performed short stories at The Exchange Bar. Helen has had poetry published in four anthologies by Poetry Now. She has two Cats.

THE LAST POST

"Late again, Niall. This is the seventh late start you've had this month. It's getting to be quite a habit. You have an alarm clock I take it?"

"Sure, normally up on time, just had a late night, sorry."

"But you've had a lot of these late nights recently. Are you acting in a play again? You seem very tired."

"Nope; just doing other stuff."

"Something bothering you at home? If you need some support..."

"No no, I'm chilled."

He resented the intrusion. She obviously had too much time on her hands; surely there were more pressing matters at the Phoenix to attend to.

"Can I get on now?" He strode to the bar. "Hi, is anybody waiting?"

"Large Americano, please."

"Sure now, be a few moments."

As he deftly operated the machine, his thoughts rose along with the steam. It was a repetitive job, but he hoped it might lead to greater things. In the meantime, he must endure it. He forced a smile.

"Thanks, sugar and milk there. Have a good day now. Who's next?"

Several hours later after many cups and plates had passed through his sore hands, Niall buttoned up his coat; relieved to be finishing his shift. He felt the script in his pocket, making sure it couldn't fall out.

Leaving the building, he breathed in the fresh air and walked along with his normal leisurely gait, absent-mindedly pulling leaves from the trees whilst whistling some indiscriminate tune. He hoped that she would be pleased to see him and not be in too much pain today.

In a few minutes he had arrived at the old lady's flat in Queen's Street. Inside it was small but warm with the comforting aromas of cinnamon, yeast and herbs. A world of lace and antimacassars, it was crammed with photographs. Dusty ornaments stood; collected from a lifetime on the stage.

"Hello? Only me." Niall shouted.

"Come through."

Keziah raised herself painfully in her chair.

"You're a good boy, thanks for coming over love."

"That's grand sure, thanks for helping with my audition for drama school."

"Have you eaten? There's nothing to you."

"I'll pick up something later, don't worry; I'm right."

Keziah took his hands in hers. "Now you must never stint on food, it's important. Promise you'll eat well tonight. "

"Okay, promise."

"There's some tea in the pot, it should still be warm. Help yourself to biscuits."

"Thanks, you know you would have made a good mother...."

There was a long silence.

She sat blinking, sipped her tea then carefully replaced her cup.

"Sorry, didn't think."

"That's alright love; it was never on the cards for me anyway but I made my choice."

"You could have found someone else after the war, people would have understood."

"I didn't want anyone else. I wanted Len. He wrote a good letter, I'll give him that."

Niall went to the beige stone mantlepiece and took up the letter with a flourish.

"You know you want me to..." he teased.

"Is it that time already?" She rejoined.

"No, no I've got stage fright!"

"Oh no, please read it to me, mellifluous voice."

"ONCE MORE WITH FEELING!" They roared in unison and laughed.

Niall cleared his throat.

"Dearest Kezzie, I'm fine, bit bored as nothing much happening, but soon we're joining the other boys who've been checking for mines, so I've got until the 21st of September to enjoy myself, ha ha. I should be alright, so don't worry. You know me; keep turning up like a bad penny, no matter what. Hope you're bearing up, I know it's hard, but I'll soon be home, then I can show you off to the world, and I've got a surprise for you. Keep me in your thoughts before you go to sleep, all my love, Len. Kisses. "

"Thanks for indulging an old lady, love."

"You're welcome." Niall swallowed hard.

"Two weeks later, he was gone, I never did get to be Mrs. Norris, but still. I have my memories. Shall we do the set pieces tomorrow? I'm a little tired now."

"Of course, sorry. Still Coriolanus' speech?"

"Absolutely, but you're top class already; you'll show 'em this time love I know it. Before you go, would you get the morphine down for me, the pain's getting to me tonight."

"Sure, no problem."

Niall located the cupboard. "There's two bottles on the top shelf at the back...." he called.

"That's right, bring both."

He returned and set them down for her. "There, will you be good now?"

"Most definitely."

"Bye then."

As he kissed her on both cheek's she held on to him for a long time. "Special boy, bless you..."

Keziah heard the door close and slowly dragged a large bottle of liquer whiskey from behind her cushion placing it next to the tablets and liquid morphine on the side table. As the light faded, she read yet again Len's fragile letter smiling to herself.

In the morning, the precious letter nestled in Keziah's chilled hand. Her smile now fixed forever.

Niall, during his break, was just going over his lines when a note slipped from the script and gently fluttered to the floor. As he stooped to pick it up, he saw that it began with a kiss.

It stated simply, 'The readiness is all.'

ANDREA WORBOYS
Moved to Leicestershire in 2018 and is comfortable with both rural and city life. She has self-published 2 children's books and is also an active member in poetry and writing groups. She has worked mainly with disadvantaged people as a tutor and a life coach, whilst coping with M.E.

MY LEICESTER ...SHIRE

Pausing at the top of the hill, I surveyed the tranquil scene. The sun, filtering through the clouds, shone on the green fields. Sheep, contentedly grazing, ignored the walkers who were sharing their right of way. The driver of the solitary car, passing through, paused, watching two young calves, friskily running around their patient mothers. Everyone appreciating the ambience in the grounds of Launde Abbey, embedded in rural Leicestershire.

Passing through the metal gate that bypasses the cattle grid, I continue down the narrow tarmac road. To my right down in the dip, nestling in the trees, is the large Elizabethan house, now ideally at home as a Retreat Centre. Although it is owned by the Church of England, all are welcome through its doors.

The original priory was founded circa 1119, by Richard and Matilda Bassett, as an Augustinian Priory. The Augustinians, were, a forward-thinking bunch, surviving on their wits and chantries!

Canon Walter Baldock deserted Dunstable for Launde Abbey. He was a plausible rogue who endeared himself with the unstable Richard II and obtained a substantial endowment for the Augustinians. Eventually, he was beheaded for treason on behalf of the king!

The chapel, including the stain glass windows, survived Henry VIII's Dissolution of the Monasteries, and can be visited to this day. Cromwell acquired the property, but never lived there. His family built, on the site, the existing seventeenth century building, and the name was changed to Launde Abbey.

Walking towards the rear of the house, I find the kitchen gardens. Surrounding these are grassy paths, an invitation to visitors to walk the extensive grounds. Before I do that, I will follow the tantalising aromas emitting from the kitchen. Coffee is being served in the coffee shop. I will indulge myself with lunch in the restaurant.

Reading the literature on the shelves, I discover that on certain days you can book an interesting talk, and lunch!

Leaving the tranquility of Launde Abbey, I head north to treat my taste buds again, in the busy market town of Melton Mowbray.

Entering the famous pork pie shop, the oldest landmark in Melton Mowbray, the cabinets are full of cheeses and pies.

Stilton cheese, very tasty with celery, takes its name from Stilton near Huntingdon, but it was never made there.

Chatting to the staff, I am asked if I know how much milk is in a 16lb Stilton cheese? I don't know. The answer is 17 gallons!

Cheese uses curd, so the whey from making the cheese is waste; this was given to feed the pigs.

The more cheese that was made, the more waste there was! Then, there weren't enough pigs to eat it all, so the farmers bought more pigs!

'Too many pigs the farmers cry, so that was the beginning of the famous pork pie'. An outlet for the pigs.

There are various creations, the most unusual being the 'New York Deli' pie, this has pastrami and gherkins through the middle, and can be exclusively bought in the pie shop.

Through the year food festivals are held to tantalise our taste buds even more. If you have a sweet tooth, you may like to know that chocolate is also included! Now on to the pulsating city of Leicester.

Walking down from the train station, towards the city centre, I find myself drawn in to the busy but easy-going air of the people going about their daily business.

The indoor market is bustling, my ears tune in to the chatter, the accentuated English mingling with their mother tongue. 'One pound, a bowl of bananas!' The colourful fruit and vegetables compete with the bolts of colour on the fabric stalls.

Coffee again! Sitting in one of the many bistros, chatting with new friends, coffee in hand, I am mesmerised by the national dress from so many countries all blending into one multicultural city. Beanies, baseball caps, turbans, rastacaps, hijabs and burkas. European versatility mixed with the vibrant colours of Asian cultures and religions.

I also discover there are museums to browse and history to explore. Where else would you find a king under a car park! There are meeting places for art and literary groups, theatre shows, music and drama.

So, whatever mood I find myself in, needing solitude or culture this is my world of Leicestershire and I'm enjoying it so very much.

SARAH KIRBY
NEW WALK MUSEUM

Sarah has lived in Leicester since becoming a member of the Leicester Print Workshop in 1991. She lives in the city centre and her work is about the world around her.... her city, her garden, her allotments. All provide a constant source of inspiration and interest. Sarah has a long term and continuing series of linocuts about the buildings in Leicester (to date over 50 images) looking at her city through its architecture, about how places are shaped by the people who live, work and pass through them and in turn contribute to a sense of place, pride and home. In 2012 /13 Sarah was awarded a Leverhulme Artist in Residence award with the University of Leicester. Working with the Centre for Urban History she made a series of works about Leicester's industrial buildings, focussing on the City's manufacturing past; the rise, fall and re-invention of a city scape. During 2018/19 she has been one of three Artists in Residence at Launde Abbey in Rutland, creating a body of work about the building and the ancient woodland around it, for exhibition at the Abbey to mark its 900-year anniversary. Recent commissions include two pieces of work for the collection of Abington Park Museum, Northampton to mark the 2018 re-launch of the Museum, tea labels for Fortnum and Mason and cover images for Candlestick Press.

TATU HENTTONEN

Is a Finnish freelance translator specialising in history and politics. He lived and worked in Leicester for six months in 2018–2019.

ONE HUNDRED THOUGHTS ON LEICESTER
SEPTEMBER 2018 – JANUARY 2019

I

At the time of writing, every Greggs in Leicester has sold out of vegan sausage rolls and super strength zombie drug has hit the streets. Sometimes a bird sings before noon. In early September, when I arrived from Finland, Abbey Park was still bustling with activity. I was impressed by people enjoying a ride on the miniature railway. It was the first time I went jogging in Leicester and, having chosen a path near the park, I was attacked by a dog from nearby tents. For some time after that, I was concerned for my safety and paid close attention to suspicious shabby residential buildings, of which there seemed to be a lot. I was staying in an area that seemed rough and then moved to another area that also seemed rough. Gradually, I realised the criteria for 'rough' were different from what I had thought, and I lowered my guard. Shabby or derelict buildings give Leicester character (and I take my hat off to the person who has filled the city with graffiti depicting worms). The city's well-kept historical buildings are impressive, of course, but to me they do not define the city, with the exception of New Walk, which might be the most idyllic spot in Leicester. The pedestrian street between Marks & Spencer and Haymarket Shopping Centre might be the least idyllic; you could almost mistake it for a Finnish shopping street. The difference between idyllic and kitsch can be slight: the Haymarket Memorial Clock Tower definitely manages to look kitsch though it probably didn't look kitsch when it was built in 1868. Before Christmas, the clock tower was decorated with heavy illuminated garlands that complemented the look nicely – so nicely that the garlands are still there now at the end of January. Streets in Leicester can be unpredictable combinations of different looks, and most of the tallest buildings seem randomly located, but everything is satisfyingly compactly built. The endless streets of old red-brick terraced houses are eye candy to me. Before I arrived, Frog Island next to the canal stood out on the map and I assumed it to be a posh neighbourhood, but it turned out to be an industrial area. Many areas in Leicester seem like they are going to be changed by gentrification. I read somewhere that the city has good economic prospects and building sites such as the Wolsey Island area overlooking the canal suggest this. My spouse's Finnish mom remembers Wolsey socks from her youth.

II

I can imagine people liking young Red Leicester in a similar way I like Edam cheese. I have bought a chunk of Stilton and a pork pie from Melton Mowbray; it was the proper thing to do. I eat less bread in Leicester than I do in Finland, mainly because I don't care for toast and I categorise Asian breads differently, and this is a healthy development. Other things I eat less in Leicester include quark, olives, pasta, gherkins, berries, bananas and sushi, all of them for different reasons. Things I eat more in Leicester include fresh spinach, oranges, fresh chillies and herbs, hummus, grapes, parsnips, frozen meat-free burgers and sausages, pies, curries, fish and chips, fried chicken and fried noodles. It seems I have started to eat more. I drink more cask ales and tea while I drink less lager and coffee. In Leicester, my love for Indian food has reached a saturation point. I like to do my grocery shopping on Sunday evenings when all the big grocery stores are closed. Food is more affordable here than in Finland and fresh ingredients taste better. The same goes for beer: it's more affordable and tastes better. I'd like to stay in pubs after midnight – apparently there are other places for late night fun, but I don't find them as pleasant. The city has many cosy, memorable pubs. Oddly, pensioners and workers seem to have a great time singing karaoke in Spencer's when I pass it by at 4 p.m. When I happened to visit Duffy's Bar during a gig, the old punkers reminded me of the places I frequent in Finland. No one seems to know why Helsinki nightclub next to the former International Hotel carries the name of my hometown, the capital of Finland; one customer said Helsinki is a town in America, 'and who cares anyway', while the owner said the nightclub was named after a factory once situated in the premises.

III

I'm under the impression that Leicester is nice but quiet. I really don't know what's happening here because I don't know anyone – I have a visitor's mentality. I find the locals very polite and friendly to strangers: for example, cyclists outside the city centre usually say 'thank you' when they pass you by, and more than one local has complimented my attire. Neither has ever happened in Finland. I don't know which feels weirder, being called a 'sir' or being called a 'mate', because in Finland we don't use any such terms of address in conversation. When I try to get to know people here, I don't know what boils down to personality and what boils down to culture. I'm thought of as a 'Finnish person'. I work from home for Finnish customers, which further weakens my ties to my surroundings. Reading the Leicester Mercury gives you a bizarre picture of the city with its emphasis on crime, violence and scare stories. The biggest piece of news about Leicester during my stay has concerned Leicester City chairman Vichai Srivaddhanaprabha's helicopter crash, which raised interest in Finland, too, because quite a lot of people in Finland know Leicester for its football team now. When a friend from Finland visited Leicester in December, she joked: 'The best bit about visiting Leicester was visiting Nottingham.' It wasn't very funny. It's hard to disagree that the various ethnic groups and their impact on the local culture make Leicester special, but she didn't single that out. For example, I never knew there could be so many late-night ice cream parlours in one city. I was looking forward to Diwali, and I was impressed by the fireworks in the Diwali lights switch-on event but underwhelmed by the dance performances. On the day before the main Diwali, a boy who lives next door kept repeating 'Diwali, Diwali, Diwali'. Later, I tried to make it to the central square for the Christmas lights switch-on event, but by the time I got there, they had already switched on the lights. I was impressed by the gigantic 'Christmas Greetings' sign on the town hall. When I heard the song 'Stop the Cavalry' for the first time in my life, I was in Morrisons. Very soon I heard it at the gym. On Christmas Day, I saw a fox entering Victoria Park.

IV

I have no idea of Richard III's place in history; my general picture of the course of events starts to get hazy from the 19th century backwards. I have a feeling the city council's emphasis on Richard III has more to do with tourism than with the local historical identity, but it's hard to tell. In the ruins of the Roman baths in Leicester, I like the surrounding brutalist buildings. I was captivated by an exhibition on Leicester's history of immigration in the 1970s. I went to a film archive screening on Leicester's past and the screening was presented by a charming old man; I could have made those screenings a weekly routine. I now realise I have learned next to nothing about the city's politics. Without conscious effort, it is possible to see that some people need to beg on the street. I read on the Internet that if you take an evening walk in the centre of Leicester, you're bound to encounter at least one weird thing, and for a while I thought this was true, but now I can't think of any other examples than lonely people shouting out loud to themselves. The city council's balance of power, with Labour holding 52 seats while the Conservatives only hold one, seems absurd in the light of the Finnish multi-party system. However, I congratulate Leicester City Council for having the smallest number of Conservative seats out of all the city councils in the UK.

V

Nowadays, I walk down New Walk in a neutral state of mind. I have grown both a little attached to and bored with my everyday surroundings. Victoria Park is important to me because I jog round it; Walnut Street is important to me because my gym is there; Swain Street Bridge is important to me because I cross it on my way to Lidl. I have learned to cross the pelican crossing on Welford Road without waiting for the lights to change on my way to Morrisons. Although I rarely feel like visiting Highcross shopping centre, I often visit it. London Road is important to me because I usually walk down it to the city centre, which takes about 20 minutes. When walking along a narrow lane, such as the Evington Footway or any path next to a concrete-walled industrial building, I think I'm in a picturesque place. When jogging by the canal, I'm afraid of falling into it. Unlike in Helsinki, pretty much everything in my daily life in Leicester is within walking distance. In Leicester, I walk more than in Helsinki, but in Leicester I don't cycle at all. The city has many pedestrian streets with a peaceful vibe to them, but the streets with cars are often the opposite of this. Irritatingly, when drivers need to give way to other cars at junctions, they stop to queue on crossings instead of giving way to pedestrians; initially I found this impolite – perhaps the only impolite thing I had come across – but now I realise it's just another way of sharing space. When walking around the city, I'm continuously completing a mental map that I want to remember for a long time. I like to observe how the different neighbourhoods meld into one another. Every area has a meaningful place in my mind: for example, it's great to know what Beaumont Leys is like, and I have now accidentally seen the largest crisp production plant in the world. Leicester's West End caught me by surprise because it was like another high street. When taking a walk in Spinney Hills, I was mesmerised by the local high street of exotic shops that appeared from nowhere. Green spaces are scarce compared to Finnish cities, but there are many meadows, and the signs next to them give an impression that the city appreciates its meadows. I thought the lakes in Watermead Country Park looked remarkable on the map, and they were pretty nice on the spot, too. However, I was confused by the fact that someone had dug so many artificial lakes there, and I couldn't find a reason for this in the signs or on Wikipedia.

VI

I'm glad my spouse got an unexpected offer to study at the University of Leicester for one semester. If her original plan to study in Taipei had worked out, I would have never visited Leicester, and I appreciate the rare opportunity. Of course, coming from an EU member state, I've been somewhat anxious about the fact that 48.9% of the people in Leicester voted to leave the European Union. I take it as a statement against me personally, but then again, they probably voted to leave for other reasons. If the government's current plans go ahead, I wouldn't be able to settle in the UK permanently with my current income after free movement ends. I'm glad I'll be leaving my flat soon because I've had many problems with it: a broken boiler, a broken gas meter, a broken fridge, a broken lightbulb socket, windows that don't open, mould caused by damp, and water dripping through the ceiling and seeping through the walls. It is a 'luxury flat'. The property manager has been quick to respond to my worries. I hope nothing serious will happen during my last month here. I regret that I will not see Leicester in midsummer. Even throughout the winter, it's possible to see plants flowering here and there and people chatting in parks before dusk. Leicester's winters are comparatively sunny. In Finland, I would have to go without sunshine for several months in a row.

LISA WILLIAMS

Was born in the West End and now lives in Clarendon Park. She is on the MA Creative Writing course at Leicester University. Lisa works part time in a bakery and although nearly 50, still has no idea what she wants to be when she grows up.

COMMUNITY

The wind blows across Victoria Park because it has nothing else to do. Simon, in his Barbour wellies and gilet from Joules likes people to see him collecting the rubbish. He will go home and photograph the contents of the bin bag later and post it on the Clarendon Park Facebook Group. It'll get three likes.
While he's tied up virtuously litter picking his unattended dog shits by a bench.
Later a toddler in red wellies, actually too tight for him, treads through the mess unseen by the Mum who is busy on her phone liking a post about litter on Facebook.
A neat circle you couldn't make up.
She posts later about the dog mess. A why-oh-why rant that attracts a lot of comments. Simon won't see the post. He'll be chatting online to a girl while his wife puts the bins out. The girl is actually an account created that afternoon by three local teenagers, they were going to go to the park, but were put off by the weather.
And so, the wind blew.

NICK PALMER

Graduated from University of Leicester and Leicester found a place in his heart. He published a poetry volume, Three Worlds, with Inspired Quill in 2012. He's written for the Leicester Comedy Festival, Spark Children's Arts Festival and RSC's Open Stages project. Lives in Scraptoft with his wonderful wife and children.

HOMECOMING

The buildings of the University dominated the skyline, striking the chords of Sarah's memory. Her relentless trudge became a determined hike. In her mind's eye she was with Katie and Surita in their first year of University. The long stretch of Queens Road before them, dipping down towards the fish and chip shop and then rising past the garage and the shops before erupting onto the vista of Victoria Park. The University, their destination, was always visible ahead of them, if only by the tip of the Attenborough Tower protruding above the turn of the century terraces.

The memory of those walks stayed with her as she made her way down the hill in the centre of the road. The tarmac was cracked and crumbling. Cars rusted in front of the houses on either side. Some cars had been abandoned; doors flung wide open. Sarah gave them all a wide birth. It would not be the first time someone had tried to take her by hiding in the boot of a car. Once or twice she had thought about taking a car instead of walking, but they were noisy and would draw too much attention. Besides, fuel was scarce: the petrol stations had long since been drained dry.

She took her water bottle from her backpack and unscrewed the top, searching the road for any signs of life. Grass grew wild through the paving stones. Weeds sprouted from the guttering of the houses, unchecked over the years. She looked with significant misgivings at the houses themselves. The windows were like eyes watching her. She hoped to be long gone before dark. If it hadn't been for the beacon, she wouldn't be here at all.

The water bottle scuffed her already chapped lips and she tasted blood. She wondered if the shops would still have supplies, but she didn't get her hopes up. Even the rural places she'd passed to get here had been looted. She remembered the winter days when she, Surita and Katie had walked into University sharing beeswax lip balm or the red and yellow stuff that Surita used that made Sarah's lips tingle. It had been easy to be free with things in those days of plenty.

She screwed the top back on the water bottle and tried not to worry about how little was left. The beacon had promised shelter and safety. She was almost out of water. She had only a few scraps of food. Hunger tore at her stomach between waking and the fitful sleep she had in the night. She had not slept properly for weeks. Walking towards the University, she could almost imagine that it was exam stress keeping her from her dreams. Almost.

The first shop she passed was nothing but toppled shelves and broken windows. Strip lights hung on exposed wires and the till lay in pieces across the cracked tile floor. A sweet stand stood empty on the counter; another had been knocked onto its side. She could see no one inside and no reason to go inside.

No corpses either. She was relieved about that. It was almost all her human contact these days. The bodies of those that didn't survive the virus. The bodies of those that had not survived the months after. The world wiped almost clean, as if by the wrath of God. Everything had failed, civilisation included.

Sarah felt the sickness rise, the burn of bile in her throat that always accompanied thoughts of the virus. Everyone had caught it. She remembered the ache in her joints that were the first symptom. Sitting at her desk in the office and feeling like someone was trying to prise her bones apart with a red-hot poker. The muscular spasms as she'd gone home on the bus, her fingers jerking out of time to music that played out in waves of pain. The fever consuming her as she'd stumbled in her hallway, the front door left open. Crawling to the bottom of the stairs before falling unconscious. No one helped her. Everyone else was sick too.

Recovery had been agony. More than once she'd wished she'd died, like everyone else had on her street. The stench of death filled her village. When she had been well enough to stand, to hobble to the window and peer out, she had seen dead parents in the playground. She had hitched the curtains shut before she had to see dead children. She tried to sleep, but she saw her neighbours' faces in her dreams. The broken blood vessels in white-filmed eyes. The skin peeling from skulls. Nightmares no worse than the world outside her door.

There had been others in her village who made it through. The survivors of Scraptoft banded together and burned the dead in the field opposite All Saint's Church. It had been called the Edith Cole Memorial Park. Now it was just the Memorial.

She had hated the work. They had all taken it in turns to collect wood and collect bodies. They took keys from the pockets of the dead, leaving keepsakes and clothes to burn. So many dead. So many of them children. After the burning, the dead left her dreams in peace. She hoped that they had found some peace of their own.

Many of the Scraptoft survivors had stayed in their houses. Some were too weak to travel. They had survived the virus, but it had taken its toll. Some stayed for their children, wanting them to grow up in houses they knew rather than on the road. Others moved away. Those who had lost family members. Those whose family members lived elsewhere but had survived. By the time Sarah left, there were only a handful of people left and supplies were dwindling every day. There had been plans to turn the area near the playground into an allotment but those had come to nothing. People grew their own food and guarded it jealously. Suspicion of neighbours became commonplace. Sarah got out before the rising tension could become killing.

She continued down Queens Road looking east, as if she could see the five miles to Scraptoft through the houses and over the land. That small village that she had made her home. She'd lived in Leicester, in the shadow of the University, since graduating. When she realised all her friends had moved away and she had no stomach for late nights out on the town, she'd decided to move somewhere with trees and fields.

She hadn't expected it to be forever, but the village was idyllic. She could sit by the duck pond and watch coots and gulls, moor hens and mallards fighting for food scattered from children's hands. She could watch buzzards quartering the fields, soaring above small flocks of sheep and cows. Songbirds flittered through the hedgerows as she walked down the lane. At dusk, bats swooped over the pond as fairy lights from the house on the opposite bank twinkled above the water. The place had lodged in her soul. It had been worse than dying watching the village she loved die. She would never go back.

She wondered if coming back to the University was the next best thing. It had been a home to her as well, before the call of village life. Her first real home in so many ways. She remembered the open day at the campus. The guide had told her that the best thing about Leicester was that it was big enough to be interesting, small enough to care. He'd been right. She had spent hours in the library and days on campus. She could picture it without effort. But there was nothing to suggest that the beacon was not a trap. There were plenty of those out on the road.

She tried to count how long she had been wandering. The tiredness, the hunger, and the thirst. The constant fear of meeting others and the desperate desire for company. Loneliness bit deeper than frost. She knew that better than most. She'd ripped her gloves in the bitter heart of winter and never found replacements. At first, the little finger of her left hand had felt like it was burning. The flesh turned black as charcoal. Then the pain became so intense, she had scavenged for a heavy knife and sterile dressings. The relief from the dull ache was better than the sharp edge of the knife. That had been eight months ago. She had never got used to her hand without the finger.

She passed the fish and chip shop. The sign hung from the side of the building, threatening to fall. The colours were washed out and streaked with dirt but it was familiar. She remembered David's birthday party: stumbling out of the house, a bottle of vodka down, and shushing the group to appease the touchy neighbours. She and David had sat together on the cheap plastic seats. She'd laid her head on his shoulder. Then, the movie-type magic. A look into one another's eyes. A kiss. The rest of the group cheered and Surita shouted 'Finally!' It seemed a lifetime ago.

The sound of metal barrels clanking together jolted her from her reverie. It reminded her of the draymen rolling barrels of beer off their truck, a balletic routine accompanied by a cacophony of clanging. Now, it meant only danger. Sarah pressed herself against the white flocking of the chip shop wall. She loosened a strap on her backpack. The hockey stick slid into her hand. She'd used it for Varsity hockey, back in the day. It served a different purpose now.

She hefted it in her hands, feeling the bitter sting of the missing finger. She had been good at hockey. She knew how to swing her stick. Controlled action. Dead on target. She checked that the knife she'd taken for her finger was still at her belt. If the worst came to the worst, she had a back-up plan.

She crept down the road, worrying that her breathing would give her away, but knowing that to hold it would only leave her gasping. The sound had not been repeated. She gave herself leave to hope that it had just been something shifting, a shelf collapsing. The large green bay doors of the garage stood open. The bottom window of the glass door was shattered and boarded with cheap plywood.

She moved in through the first bay door and scanned every corner of the testing area. One of the jacks was up. A car stood on it, cables trailing from the underside like guts. On the ground in the farthest corner a barrel rocked on the spot. The noise had come from in here. Something in her wanted to call out but she stuffed the urge down. Her eyes shifted to the door. She could be out and gone. There was nothing to stop her but her own curiosity.

She stepped towards the barrels, keeping the hockey stick held low and ready. Her eyes traced the recesses of the workshop. A clatter of tools from behind her made her turn, a strangled scream escaping her throat. Something small and black whipped past her head and out of the doors. She followed, hockey stick raised, and saw a magpie flying on faltering wings to the rooftops opposite. Just a bird. Just an injured bird.

She retreated into the cover of the workshop and let the wall take her weight. Her breath came in ragged gulps and her heart pounded in her ears. She focused on her breathing, slowing it down, helping her body to recover. The magpie had rattled her. It was just a bird, she told herself as she stepped back out onto the street, but she didn't put the hockey stick away. Going armed was comforting.

The road rose ahead of her, past the closed down banks, past sandwich shops and the bus stop. The butchers was a mess. Glass was strewn across the pavement, blood streaks dried on what was left of the windows. She hoped it was from looted meat. The glass tinkled and cracked as it crushed beneath her feet. The florists was dark. Some of the plants left outside had died, others had bloomed, reaching almost to the top of the awning above.

Visions of her life here flashed in front of her eyes. Shopping with Surita for fancy dress in the charity shops before the Halloween party. Having lunch with Katie in the pizza place with the weird name. Arguing with David in the street outside the grocers. The houses of friends in the web of streets beyond, the parties and the movie nights all flooding back to mock her in this wasteland.

She'd had enough. She started to run. Running from the visions towards the park and the University beyond. It was stupid. If there was anyone here, they'd see her well before she saw them, if she saw them at all. Her legs were already tired from walking. Blisters pulled at her heels. It was a waste of energy when she had so few supplies.

But still she ran.

Across the road and onto the park. The grass grown wild and tall, hemming her in. The tarmac path cracked and sprouting shoots of its own. She walked along the bike path, which seemed clearer, and wished that it didn't feel like a transgression. There weren't cyclists to complain anymore.

She'd have liked to have found a bike. They were better than cars. They drew less attention, needed no fuel, and could help her travel further each day. If the beacon was a bust or a trap, she would hunt for a bicycle.

The thought of the beacon slowed her down. She broke off from the run, sweating and desperate for water. She drained the last from her bottle. Water, food and a bike. The same shopping list she'd had when she'd moved to University for the first time. She'd never got around to getting the bike. Her student loan hadn't stretched that far.

As the path ahead turned, she saw the University properly for the first time. The Attenborough Tower, affectionately nicknamed the Cheese Grater, thrusting into the sky. The squat and hunched form of the Charles Wilson Building sitting solid ahead of her. The Engineering Building, a work of architectural significance with very expensive windows. The sun reflected off the glass frontage of the Library, that devoid of atmosphere cube in which she'd spent so many hours. She hadn't missed the Library.

She left the path and entered the gates. The black railings were rusted, and the borders had grown out. The stems of the plants waved in the breeze. Sarah relaxed her grip on the hockey stick and then remembered that this could all be a trap. She gathered her wits and moved into the shadow of the Tower.

She walked through the underpass and climbed the stairs. The Centenary Square spread out before her, the site of a thousand interactions and the most treasured of her memories. Sitting with her friends, watching the world go by. It was empty now, rain-streaked and gloomy. She skirted it and tried the doors of the Students' Union. Locked tight.

Almost by instinct, she headed towards the Sports Centre, a walk she had made so many times before. To her left the Fielding Johnson Building stood, Georgian grandeur still evident despite the scars of the intervening years. From the flagpole, the University colours flew, red against the iron sky. The doors would be locked, but she went to try them anyway.

They folded open as she approached. She stood shocked as they moved. They were powered. She hadn't seen anything electrical working in years, not so much as a light bulb. She hesitated, wondering whether to run. Tightening her grip on her hockey stick to gather her courage, she stepped in through the doors into a luxurious reception area. It was almost exactly as she remembered it, except for the large table placed in the centre of the space. There was a man behind the table, with papers in front of him. Two large men wearing fluorescent jackets marked 'SECURITY' stood to either side.

"Welcome," the man behind the table said,

"Please sit. My name is Rob."

He indicated a chair in front of the table. Sarah cast a suspicious eye over them as she sat down. No women. She had come across gangs of men on the road and they had never had good intentions. Sarah rested the hockey stick in easy reach and loosened the knife in its sheath. With surprise on her side, she might make time to run. She gave her first name, steeling herself for her escape.

"Have you been to the University before?"
Rob asked, folding over a page on the clipboard in front of him and clicking a biro in his left hand.

"I studied here," she said,

"Graduated two years before the virus."

"We'll have to check our records,"
Rob said, marking something down on the clipboard,

"How did you find us?"

"There was a beacon. Picked it up on an old radio I found. Heard it was safe, that there might be shelter, food, water."

She croaked the words out. Her throat ached. This was the most talking she'd done since leaving the village. One of the security guards brought her water in a pitcher and a clean glass, as though she was here for an interview. Sarah stared at it before lifting the pitcher in shaking hands. Fresh water sources were few and far between on the road.

"We have all of those things here," Rob said,

"You can be safe here."

Sarah paused, the glass touching her lips. She didn't drink. She wasn't sure what was in the water.

"Are there any women here?" she asked, "In positions of authority?"

"Of course," Rob said, hand already waving her question aside.

"I'd like to meet some."

Rob smiled and nodded to one of the security guards. Sarah's hand closed around her knife handle, but the security guard made for the stairs at the back of the room. He jerked his head in a 'follow me' gesture. Sarah rose, her hand still on her knife handle and her other gripping the hockey stick. No one seemed to care about her weapons, but they had no idea how well she could use them.

She edged around the table, trying to keep all of them in sight. She knew she must look skittish and suspicious but that was okay. Let them think her more scared than she was. It might give her an advantage. She followed the security guard up the stairs, crab-walking up each step so she could watch the others. Neither of them moved. Only the security guard watched her go. Rob looked at his paperwork, leafing through the scattered papers without concern.

At the top of the stairs, they passed through some double doors with glass panels smashed out of them. Sarah kept back from the security guard as he knocked on one of the doors. The sound echoed in the room beyond and then he went in. With no other choice, Sarah followed.

The room beyond was huge and Sarah noted that the two sets of doors both led to this room. There were white tables with chairs arranged around them. She could have been walking into a seminar. At a grand, wooden desk, there was a woman. She was towards the end of her middle years, with a prominent nose and a slightly crooked smile. Her light brown hair was short and there were pearl earrings in each ear. She sat hunched, her neck forward of her shoulders, giving her the appearance of a bird.

"Sorry to interrupt, Vice-Chancellor. We had an arrival and she wants to meet women in authority." Said the security guard.

"Very wise," the Vice-Chancellor said, rising from the chair and walking over to Sarah. She seemed even more bird-like in motion. She offered Sarah her hand.

"Pleased to meet you."

"I thought all Vice-Chancellors were old, white men," Sarah said, ignoring the hand and gesturing to the portraits on the wall.

"Often," the Vice-Chancellor said, "but not always. Things do change and are changing. Come with me."

The Vice-Chancellor led them through the function room and down a corridor opposite. There were rooms off either side of the corridor, regularly spaced, and Sarah remembered that the Fielding Johnson Building was once the Leicestershire and Rutland Lunatic Asylum. It had the feel of an asylum still.

They took more turnings and Sarah lost her bearings. She wondered if the complexity of the route was deliberate. Her hand tightened on the hockey stick. The Vice-Chancellor led them into a long corridor. It reminded Sarah of the kind used in stately homes as art galleries. In here, there were no portraits of men on horseback with silly haircuts. Instead, beds lined the walls, like a field hospital scene from a war movie.

"One of five wards," the Vice-Chancellor said,

"We are hoping to expand to other buildings soon to make more space."

The Vice-Chancellor continued to explain her plans for the future of the institution, but Sarah was not listening. She was looking at the back of a woman sitting beside one of the beds. The auburn curls were more than familiar, even without seeing her face.

"Katie?" Sarah said.

Katie turned and recognition blossomed on her face. She looked exactly as Sarah remembered her except for a scar across her left eyebrow and a haunted look in the eyes. Sarah wondered if her eyes had that look. Katie smiled and pulled Sarah into her arms.

"When did you get here?"

"Just now. You?"

"Surita and me, we came in a few weeks ago."
Katie said, gesturing to the bed.

Surita lay in the bed, her eyes closed and her skin tinged grey. The images of the Scraptoft dead rose to Sarah's mind.

"Is she okay?"

"She will be now," Katie said,

"If the security guards hadn't found us..."

She let the consequences go unsaid. Sarah's hand found Katie's and she squeezed it for reassurance. She never wanted to let that hand go. Tears welled in her eyes.

"We try to patrol to find survivors," Said the Vice-Chancellor.

"We turn no one away, if their intentions are good. We want to be a haven. You'll all be safe here."

"Why?"
Sarah asked the Vice-Chancellor, tears still coming,

"Why the beacon? Why save us?"

"We were founded by one broken generation for the benefit of the next," the Vice-Chancellor said,

"Some things are worth keeping alive. Our motto has become our purpose."

The Vice-Chancellor gestured to the window. Sarah saw the University colours fluttering on the flagpole. They were more than a red blur this time. She saw the gold outline around a red shield, the silver cinquefoils of the city and the golden horseshoe. Between them was an open book, inscribed with the motto.

She could just make the words out as the flag waved.
Ut vitam habeant. So that they may have life.

SARAH KIRBY
BLUNTS

ROSA FERNANDEZ

Is a writer and poet based in Leicester. She studied English at Goldsmiths and can be very funny, but only for those with low expectations. She enjoys wearing hats, being heartily socialist, and thinking about biscuits. Crumbs!

PAINT STOPS: A LEICESTER TAG-ELOGUE

I walk a clockwise loop around the city, looking to take in some familiar names. My bag is stocked with invisible cans; I plan to leave a memory of myself in all my significant places, but I'm still deciding what form my tag will take. I'm looking out for WRS, and I'll be exploring RELMS. One, two, TROIS pops up on boards I'm walking past. I'll be unearthing some Wormsy faces. I might even prick some EGOS.

They are all here, chattering alongside each other. I like to wonder who comes, and when, and why. I wonder if AURIS has the big wide shoulders of his confident A. Does WRS dress in skinny jeans and lean? Is TROIS a visitor from Europe and does she have the long eyelashes of her seductive O? There's a sweet street democracy at work here and I enjoy the energy and immediacy of their traces. I'd rather see a purple streak on the side of a bus stop than a collection of fag ends; some are more courageous in what they leave for others to admire.

Upon visiting the Tigers they are silent, sated by the butchery at Morrisons, itself having torn through the cattle market. Meandering up Oxford Street and this one is not so busy with shoppers, just bus-stoppers in parenthesis outside the Royal Infirmary. I'd leave my initials here in a light feather blue; for the souls about to leave (and the brand-new voices) and I pass quietly with grace and reverence. At the castle, that is all dungeon and the hospital, both sets of people look back at the other, feeling pity for the inmates.

I guess on the inside of both there are a fair few words up on the wall; NOW WASH YOUR HANDS.

I approach the Swan across from the Bowling Green, but sadly it does not choose to flap and waddle to meet the other. Past the Jain Centre, where I weave through the pillars and peek through the glass. I decide that this edifice needs no more decoration; I'll save the jewel colours for the greyer parts of town. I'll find a spot to draw the hand with the wheel; the wheel as the resolution of the wandering in the pursuit of compassion. I'll wave back at the city with enlightened palms.

After the aquarium fins of a university Law School, I cannot read the Magazine. Jamie Vardy is on fire behind me, while a painted Buddha smiles beyond, free from any Millstone at the Lane. Where punk rock once smashed in the back room of The Charlotte a tiny supermarket now politely hums, and this noisy juncture is where I find all the signatures of Leicester's artists in the hole below an abandoned building. Wormsy has a speech bubble here and VIA replies; as do RELMS, KRU and a host of other writers I cannot quite decipher. To look is to find, and our furnished streets are full of signs, and signs upon signs, and stickers. Many write, but few are published. The city is full of sketches; I'm just trying to get it down somewhere before it moves.

And now I have places to be; I'm heading Southgates, whereupon St Nicholas draws his own Circle, past the castle, past Caesaranieri. Behind him the face of an uncoloured Wormsy peeks out towards the Roman ruins. The Romans bathed here, and the Romans scrawled: somewhere the words Nihil durare potest tempore perpetuo will have been worn away by time (because nothing can last forever or can it?). I look out for a fresh VIA tag to complete this Latin scene, but I catch none, and soon I am approaching a High Cross-roads.

From the circle to a square and an advert break to look up at the Cathedral spire, like a broadcast tower above the radio players. The peregrines lurk on the other side, sacrificing the odd pigeon to a higher admirer. Wyggeston House leans and winks back at Alfred Lenton, silent today but curiosity filled; books in every direction but shelves studded with almost forgotten logos on ancient boxes, a bounty for the time traveller who needs to invest in some cutting-edge film equipment.

The High Street writes a line down to the Clock Tower, surely the truest face of Leicester; implacable, timely. I know if I followed this diversion that above the stores, I'd see more traces, and more remnants. Somewhere on a high wall it says CHEMISTS BY EXAMINATION and FOR HEADACHE DRINK SEA BREEZE and I remember how far inland we are. You can see for miles from the top of Leicester, but the coast is still off the edge of the page.

In the present I have no need of the time, so I reach right out of the Mosh pit and see a sky full of cranes ahead; I gamble my way down Vaughan Way towards a giant hall of mirrors where there is no escape from reflection. I find no letters or names here, apart from those that are taller than me and halfway up the wall: John Lewis has tagged itself in spectacular style, above a hole that burrows into the earth and breathes out cars. Above the whizzing road is the rope bridge of Leicester, the crossing that seems too flimsy, the greenhouse that grows carparkers, who walk through the sky to worshop at the High Cross of consumer heaven.

Back on earth and Causeway Lane opens a chasm between sets of supplicants; plenty on one side for the altars of trinkets and none for the National Spiritualist Church, possibly only thronged with vapours now, like the vampires that drained the Blood Donor Centre whose lettering still stains the building. A few steps along, past a WRS in a doorway and I glance to another scrawl on a wall. I take a Blake Walk to a single white word on bricks: FREEDOM, and I wonder who is asking for what here? Not a signature but a request, but I see no chains in this alley, just a chicken box and the green glass remains of a good time.

I divert further upstream to The Salmon pub, closed this early but home to another joyful expression. UNSPOILT BY PROGRESS says the window and I wonder on how true that ever is; progress is change and change makes new and I don't know if I want to live in a world unspoiled. The spoiling is part of the fun, surely? The patient beauty of this tucked away sentiment is undeniable, and I head back to the main road.

On my feet like this on a morning of drizzle I see few other people and I feel like a single ant in a world full of rabbits. A boy in a t-shirt with a smudge on his face suddenly appears before me and says, "where's the shop?" and I ask which shop he means. Any shop, apparently, and I point him towards town. He fades into the droplets. I could be leaving my initials everywhere and there would be no-one to challenge me. I consider tagging the nearest corner with the words ANY SHOP while I wait for the cars to stop.

Across Church Gate and the ground opens up again. Into the subway I delve. EGOS has been here, in several colours, and HURL has hurled paint. Through the darkness to the other side I see the giant word BIN. All have bin here and some have left their mark, and I emerge from the mixed messages to the surface. There are marks above ground too, and bigger letters: from this corner it is clearly safe to SHOUT back at the church for salvation. Save me, father, for I have scrawled.

St Margaret is the patron saint of the bus station, and I can only see the local side from here; the turquoise Arrivals waiting to sail the tributaries of the city, while the big white whales to London stalk the other side. Maybe these writers come from other cities; perhaps there are RELMS in Bristol and Notts? The country a graffito puzzle where the challenge is to connect the dots.

I'm nearly at the top of the teardrop and AURIS appears on white wall by a billboard: coming soon to a grey rectangle near you! Round the brick corner and a metal fire escape and RELMS, EGOS and WRS keep company with others. I can't fly over Burley's flyover but what's mine is definitely in YOURS, so I refuel and take a simmer in one of their giant pans. I leave my fingerprints on the glass of the cake counter and leave with a bag full of sweets.

Up St Matthew's Way and traffic roars; I cannot simply ESCAPE R ALITY but instead play a balance game with myself above the dipped pavement. A Suez Canal haircut can be obtained on the other side, and I guess this must only be in the military style. I know a Phoenix is sleeping somewhere, about to rise on the horizon, but I see another Wormsy on Bray & Bray. AURIS has dug in here too, it seems. Maybe I know these people? I find their names in the places I go. I could try and trace them but that would destroy the spell. (I'm pretty sure the local police are looking for them as well.)

A Lidl further. St George's Way and the Phoenix finally shakes out her wings on the right, above the fiery colours of a HOMBOOG painted wall. This is no tag, this is art at full size, and I can only compete in my imagination. Up the side streets I see the painted sides of the Soundhouse sing the blues and the lines of the Curve run parallel, but I keep to the home straight.

I give myself a final BOOST, up the slow graceful rise to where the Ibis wades. A knight of Hastings looks down on where the railway disappears down towards the capital. The old police station looks across to the great blue Premier (like a) ship on the horizon. I don't know the how, but The Y opens its arms to those in need, and I take a moment to be stationary at the station, looking up to Thomas Cook, but I feel this travel has its own agency. The station is its own reward for those who like letters; the beautiful DEPARTURE above the arch. There is ART in DEPARTURE.

Back down Granby Street I leave behind the BLUNT red letters of the shoe shop, for so long unfixed; the letter S a ghost leaving only HOES. S has been reinstated but Leicester will hardly notice; tempting to shinny up and make it SNOBS HUSTLE and see how long it takes the city to work it out.

I press on. I cannot walk up Waterloo Way, as I have my reservations about the central reservation. I take my chances up the pavement and approach the New Walk (same as the old walk, and no cycles) and pass up the Museum to cross Regent Road, where on a corner a wedding cake building waits for a bridal party. When passing in darkness this one glows blue and almost hovers, rising from below the pavement like a spaceship docking. But now is daylight and the pristine wall is a blank exam paper waiting to be turned over and filled. It's a race down to the try line and the green freedom of Nelson Mandela Park.

I shall lay down on the cool grass after a hang off the climbing frame and try to decide what my daubs should stand for. Maybe just a symbol, like an upside-down teardrop-shaped ring road. If I stand at the bottom and I spread my paint wide, maybe I can turn all this into one giant exclamation. My mark shall only be seen from the sky.

PAM THOMPSON

Pam Thompson is a poet, reviewer and creative writing tutor based in Leicester. Her publications include The Japan Quiz (Redbeck Press, 2009) and Show Date and Time, (Smith | Doorstop, 2006). Pam has a PhD in Creative Writing and her second collection, Strange Fashion, was published by Pindrop Press in 2017. Pam is a 2019 Hawthornden Fellow.
Web-site pamthompsonpoetry@wordpress.com

OLD JOHN

Proud of its shape,
a crenellated tankard on a ridge,
it can be seen from all over the city,

It prefers early mornings
when the deer are huddled
in the wood behind Lady Jane Grey's house
where they still behead the oaks
and the only people
are volunteers in yellow cagoules.

It wants to tell us –
A tower stands vigilant through the seasons
A tower may be listed but can never be possessed
A tower is a watchdog
A tower is forever

On Armistice Day, it bears witness
to the slow climb of old people
wearing poppies, the bowing of heads at 11am.
It would like to tell them how, at sunset,
every soldier's name on the memorial catches fire.

Its ancestors were underwater volcanoes.
Surrounding rocks, carboniferous forests.
It guards the Precambrian fossil,
etched like a fern in one of its walls.

Families peer inside.
Sometimes they enter,
climb the spiral staircase
find the windows shuttered
the slate fireplace, cold.

Its heart, though,
beats through stone.

JENNIFER WORSWICK IRVING-BELL

Is an aspiring young author who writes in her spare time. Her interests include geology, philosophy and Contemporary English Literature. She has always been surrounded by nature from a young age and is appreciative of its beauty and particularly enjoys analyzing the impact of human interaction within the natural world.

WINTER'S WARMTH

Winter's warmth
Winters cruel, cold, and callous in its nature but us humans don't always let it despair. We make the most of time. It's fleeting like an hourglass turning and times running through our grasp. Robins dominate the broken branches and glaze ice. Red reflecting admiration to the slender fingers of Jack Frost. Calling its sweet melodies to welcome visitors staying for the day. They walk around the gardens puffing smoke out of their mouths like the dragons you hear of in a childhood fairy-tale. Smiles on awe-struck faces, blinded by the beauty of the Castle Gardens these robins take refuge in. Around midday they all go to the tea room, the warmth, and cup a bowl of hot soup to exile the coldness they've collected in the day. Afterwards they ponder looking around, always picking out the colours in the evergreens: red in the holly bush, and pure white snow drops. But then they leave, times slipped out of grasp again and all that's left is the trodden snow and crisp memories spent of the day in the Castle Gardens. Days, hours, minutes, seconds, time slips away and the seasons are changing. The robins migrate to a distant land and the other shrubs and lush greens begin to bloom into vibrant colours of red, yellow, and blue. The people return but this time with little ones like foals if you will. They wear summer colours like the garden, flourishing in the beauty surrounding them. Floral landscapes and green lush grass to gaze upon. The seasons are juxtaposing one another but never, ever could exhaust the true beauty of Leicester.

LARA STEEL

Is aged 16. She has lived in the Charnwood Forest area for nine years. Lara particularly enjoys writing satirical prose, often from the perspective of slightly unpleasant characters.

NOTES FROM A RAMBLING REPORTER

Objective: Report on the Charnwood Forest preferably having visited it.
Publication: Don't Shoot the Weekly Messenger.
Reporter: Yours Truly.
Specific Instructions: none.

My rambling expertise being something I pride myself upon, I set about packing a suitably-weighted rucksack containing only the bare essentials: water, emergency rations, mobile phone, electric toothbrush, luxury hand soap, portable Wi-Fi connection and, crucially, magnetic board games, as well as a few bits of elementary hiking gear including ropes, an altitude- sensitive watch, a sundial and numerous pieces of string for measuring distances. Blister plasters added but a few grams to the package, and insoles slotted discreetly into my boots. Now all that remained was to deposit myself at the intended grid reference.

My primary instinct upon arrival was to make a beeline for the nearest café for a compulsory dose of calories. I entered with confidence for, of course, I would never have embarked on such an expedition without first doing my research. Having consulted numerous sites listing examples of Leicestershire dialect and their unlikely translations, I think I could easily have been mistaken for a native.

"Ey up, me ducks. A bit parky, innit? But nowt to ge' mardy abou', 'at's what oi reckon."
The blank stares this induced only encouraged me,
"Ya wanna go down tahn or down't jitteh, cuz I'm, like, a propah Lestah chisit, I am, nowt less."
"Good morning",
said my acquaintance of recent behind the counter,
"What can I get you?"

Determined not to crumble in the face of a straightforward greeting, I ordered a Melton Mowbray pork pie with a side of Red Leicester (substituted later for a cup of tea) before "going toilet" and suitably refreshed, taking to the winding footpaths of Charnwood Forest.

The ensuing afternoon, I distributed myself over a notable few square kilometres, gracing the likes of Swithland Wood and Beacon Hill with my presence. However, it was Bradgate Park that I first visited. It occupied a vast swathe of land, most of which I managed to cover, mood and appreciation for the landscape only slightly dampened by a stitch in the abdomen and an unscheduled contact with the ground having tripped over a bit of protruding rock. Despite myself, I developed something of an engrossment in interesting foliage, much of my attention and, on occasion, torso, was consumed by the surrounding sea of bracken. Of further interest were the geological formations, great protrusions of Precambrian rock dating back 560 million years. Formed under circumstances I would struggle to describe to a subject uneducated in such areas. Of course, in my case, the exposed basement rock and prior volcanic activity were but preliminary observations.

Also surrounding the park is a history of relative interest to the amateur historian. It had been the humble abode of Lady Jane Grey from birth to the age of ten before she moved to London. All of six years later, she found herself on the throne between, allow me to consult my very intricate mental timeline, July the 10th and 19th 1553. She was swiftly beheaded, which, if nothing else, explains the briefness of her reign as it can't be easy ruling a country without a head. Which was a bit of a shame, really. Likewise and this really is riveting stuff, Beacon Hill, which I will come to describe in due course, carries with it a rich history as a signaling point used to commemorate important national events.

Now, there is a sort of unspoken rule that Bradgate Park consists of two separate pedestrian routes or 'zones.' One smoothly paved with a tearoom and, crucially, public toilets, and the other for those of greater rambling expertise and thus perfectly content to go straight into the long grass. I had so far scaled the latter and had had an admirable time doing so, but time was getting on.

I had booked myself in for a 'Venison Tasting Session' at twelve o'clock-one of the many events held by the park throughout the year, which I could only imagine involved the tasting of venison. In short, I had planned my route so that both 'sectors' of the park were visited before this time, so I really had to get a move on.

I embarked upon this second phase and was soon met with a swarm of casual pedestrians, imposing-looking dogs connected via short leashes to almost every hand such that they could have been mistaken for part of their anatomies. A number of brave souls, evidently capable of advanced coordination, also had with them a child, most of which could also have done with being attached to a short leash. Countless orders and complaints were being issued to said infants in what seemed like an inescapable stream:

"Your new trainers are covered in grass stains, Chloe",

"Sam, what have you done with the baby?"

"I don't think the duck wants to ride the bike, Jayden."

"If you're going to attack your brother like that, Ella, at least use something more robust than a twig."

I felt particularly sorry for the parents of Noah, who had closely acquainted himself with the park's underwater residents. Taking a brand-new white shirt and the dog with him before re-emerging and emptying the contents of his wellingtons, including a tadpole and some green slime of unknown origin, into his mother's handbag.

Now, for those of you with a particular interest in deer. I am sure you will not attempt to deny it. I regret to inform you that the remainder of the Midlands will leave you largely disappointed. However, the creatures accumulate in their masses at Bradgate, dispersed across many an acre, a great number of which can be observed from the relative safety of the footpath. In fact, this is true to such an extent that I feel justified, even compelled, in making the following statement: should you, and this is common, ever feel deprived of deer, visiting here will leave you satisfied for life. In my case, it was not until I had done so that I had actually seen one up close. I found them highly attractive, relative to the surrounding wildlife i.e. children and it quite captivated me to watch them forage about amongst the bracken and… do whatever it is that deer do all day. 'Elegant', I believe is the word that best describes them- long-legged and graceful. Silent too, not ones for gratuitously emitting loud wails, chirps, howls or requests for ice-cream. In short, they were beautiful creatures for which I felt a deep sympathy, as you have likely inferred.

A reminder sounded on my mobile and I glanced at my watch, it was approaching twelve o' clock: venison tasting time!

Later, I emerged from the session sufficiently fueled for the remainder of my expedition. It distressed me, initially, to transition so seamlessly from observing and marveling at to consuming the things. But upon first tasting the dish, I abandoned all concern in favour of a hearty chunk of pie, the recipe for which I have obtained in the hope that it might feature in the next issue of 'Don't Shoot the Weekly Messenger', and I might gain something financially from that.

The second trail was Beacon Hill, which put you up against an upwards incline, followed by a downwards decline, leading you back to your original location at the bottom of the upwards incline. It was undeniably a hill, and a pleasant one to scale at that. The gradient is generally gentle, rendering it a suitable place for a leisurely stroll with the family and dog, for the more ambitious amongst you, guiding you through both tunnels of woodland and across open heath exhibiting geological formations not at all unlike those of Bradgate Park. It was a thoroughly respectable place, and before I start sounding like a National Trust guidebook advertising 'fun family days out', I will proceed to discuss another of the park's unique features: the many wooden chainsaw sculptures, generously distributed about the site. Artistic prowess was certainly evident; however, I would rather not have encountered such figures on a dark night.

On the subject of frightening characters, children, of which there were far fewer than at Bradgate, were kept sufficiently occupied by a strategically-placed adventure playground, distracting them from their usual schemes, which, had their attention not been seized by the wooden labyrinth, they would doubtless have been hatching. Thus, I whipped up and back down the hill in relative peace. There wasn't even a queue for the ice-cream van!

A mere trek of a few hundred metres up the road leads you to Swithland Wood. I consider it entirely possible for the reader to infer from the place's title, the general nature of the landscape. In the event that my optimism has been misplaced, I refer to the striking abundance of trees. Now, I admit that I was slightly apprehensive due to the recalling of past experience, which has led me to view the combination of thick autumn leaf fall, tree roots, rabbit holes and dogs, post-mealtime, as a somewhat unfavourable one. However, with its being a registered public footpath and my experience thus far being largely respectable, I could rest reasonably assured that there weren't going to be any mantraps.

The walk itself was undoubtedly picturesque, as were the two previous, whilst displaying an entirely different sort of landscape and showcasing the county's diversity of countryside. There was a network of paths, meandering about in no immediately apparent direction, and the place took on an almost fairytale-like atmosphere, such that I slightly regretted not thinking to drop stale white bread along the way to mark my path instead of feeding it to the ducks. It was also remarkably quiet and serene, with my happily coming across notably more sheep than children.

As you may or may not have gathered, it was all very nice to look at. In fact, absorption in my physical surroundings lead me to neglect my intended route and journey slightly off-piste. I was in a thoughtful state over what sort of language would impact the reader the most in my article when I made sudden, solid contact with a metal post, soon identified as that of a road sign indicating the proximity of Loughborough City, or some such place. I took that as a clear indication that it was time to turn back, so did so, keeping up the pretence that I had a vague idea of where I was.

By the time my ramblings ceased, and I arrived at my nightly accommodation, the light was slipping away. It was a humble establishment, embellished externally by what looked like several square feet of Bradgate turf tacked affectionately to a vertical surface, but with the added bonus of a built-in pub named something along the lines of 'The Duckling's Head' or 'The Perturbed Deer'.

I entered said building and checked in, taking care to foresee any later requirements, previous ignorance had led me to rattle up to reception, bruised all over, asking for a non-slip bath mat, before trudging up to my room, fatigued by the day's walking. Having unlocked the door, an activity arguably more strenuous than the entire day's rambling I homogenised with the bed, my appreciation for a soft surface enhanced by the recollection of my earlier fall.

And thus, I drifted into a deep slumber, confident that the readers of my column would soon be flocking to Charnwood Forest, sufficiently clued-up on the area's points of interest and wildlife.

NICOLA ALLEN

Works in a comms and information role for a Trade Union. A part-time freelance writer and storyteller. She hopes to make writing her full time career. She lived in Leicester for a year and it is still one of her favourite places.

LEICESTER – A MEMORY

We turn the corner and see a parking space right outside the house. Number 6, Browning Street. It looks exactly the same. The front door is still painted blue, although I know it must have been repainted many times since it was my front door. "This is it," I say aloud, as much to reaffirm it in my own mind as to tell my boyfriend Jake who has driven for five hours to get us here, "my old student house."

I think about the day that my new housemates and I chose our bedrooms. We all knew as soon as we walked into the house which room we each wanted, and we all wanted different rooms - a definite sign that this was the right home and we were the right people. I chose the upstairs middle room, the window looking out onto the lanes behind the house. Directly across the way there was a shadow which always looked as though there was someone in the house opposite watching over me. Some people thought it was creepy, but somehow it brought me comfort. I was 18 years old and had never really been away from home before. This felt like a long, long way from home.

We get out of the car. I want to get going straight away, there is so much to see. Walking past the red brick terrace we turn the corner onto Barclay Street, tree lined, leaves falling to the ground, just as I remember. I pass the familiar houses of old friends and pause outside number 15. That was your house. The thought of you still gives me butterflies. I long for what might have been and looking at Jake here by my side, immediately feel guilty.

The next stop is Narborough Road, still full of takeaways, shops and bars; the hustle and bustle of today's students enjoying the last of the autumn sunshine. They look so young, surely they're not old enough to be drinking – did we look like that too? I walk a little more, a children's park is now a housing estate, a favourite café now a well-known supermarket chain. I sink a little inside, a sign of our times.

Across another road and I am back on campus, Leicester De Montfort University. I was the first person in my family to go to Uni; everyone was so incredibly proud of me although it soon became apparent that there was a definite hierarchy among Leicester students. Originally a polytechnic, DMU carried a bit of a stigma and it felt like students of the 'real' Leicester University looked down on us. I didn't care, to me the freedom of this new place, of being a real adult was exhilarating. I was filled with hopes and dreams for the life that was ahead of me and the person that this place would make me.

I stand in front of the student union building beaming as I recall the weekly Cyber cheese event, named after its obligatory midnight chips and cheese snack to soak up all the alcohol. I long for the days where I could drink like that and remain hangover free. Apparently the SU housed the longest bar in the whole of Europe. No one I met ever knew quite where that urban legend came from or whether it was true, it was certainly a good selling point though.

I wander around the site, the buildings so familiar yet less grand than I remember. The Kimberlin library, the Queens building, the Hawthorn building, they all seem smaller somehow. I am heartened to see that the Soar Point, our beloved campus local still exists and still buzzes with the energy of students grabbing a quick refreshment break between lectures. Unable to resist, I suggest that Jake and I pop in for a quick drink, it still feels like home, but I am keen to move on.

Sadly, the James Went building where I studied is no more, I smile as I realise that it may not be a bad thing – it wasn't very pretty. A 1960s high-rise, grey, uninspiring and typical of the architecture of that time. Ugly on the outside but the inside was always full of laughter. It was here I set up my very first email account. Although we could only email each other when we were in the building we still thought we were technological revolutionaries. The computer lab became a place of excitement and discovery; the Internet opening up a whole new world.

I remember how you would distract me from my studies by sending me links to your favourite bands. I became so familiar with the guitar riffs of A, the indie vibes of the Candyskins, the mellow tones of Sophie Ellis-Bextor in her first band The Audience. We would send song lyrics back and forth to one another, line by line, until someone got a word wrong. The penalty always the same – to cook dinner and do the dishes that night.

My heart beats a little faster just thinking about it and I know that just beyond the underpass is the place that I am most excited to see, the Charlotte. The place where I fell in love with live music, where I fell in love with you and where I fell in love with Leicester.

I know it's no longer a music venue; that changed a long time ago. Friends told me that it closed for a while before being turned into a gastro pub, but that didn't survive either. Naively I am not at all prepared for what awaits me, and it brings a shocked sadness, like being punched in the stomach. Student flats. Holding back the tears, I sigh. Jake tries to take my hand, but I pull away, I can't hold anybody else's hand here.

I think about the people who live here now, many of them unlikely to have been born when I was a student. I wonder if they know the history of this iconic building, the music that was played here and the bands that visited on their way to stardom. So many happy memories created here, our favourite place. Although over 20 years ago, it feels like yesterday. I cast my mind back.

It was the 7th October 1997, the day of three firsts – the first time I met you, the first time I went to the Charlotte and my first gig. All of them changed my life and all of them cemented Leicester in my heart forever.

The morning of the 7th was quite uneventful and after popping to the shop to get some milk, I had settled down in my room to do some reading. After a few hours I heard voices downstairs and being nosey decided to come and say hello. There you were, you were on the same course as my housemate and had come over to do some work. I am not ashamed to admit I fancied you like mad.

We hit it off immediately and as soon as you found out I was Welsh you launched into an enthusiastic sales pitch about your new favourite band, Stereophonics. I had never heard of them, you couldn't believe it and told me that they were playing that night in somewhere called the Charlotte. You decided that we must go. In the days before online booking we tried to call the venue but couldn't get an answer.

"Let's go down there," you said, "there are bound to be tickets left."

So, we did. I can still remember your face when we arrived and saw the big 'sold out' sticker plastered across the poster. You looked wounded.

Unsure what to do, we hung around for a while and were just about to leave when the side door opened, and three men walked out.

"It's them," you said, "I'm going to say hello."

So, you did, and even though I still didn't have a clue about the band and would usually have run a mile from situations like this, so did I. You made me brave. The conversation that followed made me a lifelong fan of the 'Phonics.

They soon picked up on the Welsh lilt in my voice and clearly feeling a little homesick were keen to have us at the gig. I remember feeling excited but wary as we gave our names for the guest list. They told us to come back later and guaranteed we would be allowed entry. I hoped so, for your sake more than anything. We went back to the student union for a drink while we waited. I found a public phone and called my mum to tell her all about what had happened and insisted that she must look out for this new Welsh band.

"They are going to be huge," I said.

Of course, at this point I still hadn't heard any of their songs, but your passion was infectious. I remember hearing my mum laugh as she said,

"Give it a year or two and you won't even remember who they are."

As I write this, 22 years later I am very proud to say that they are still a very present part of my life and that I was right, they are huge. I have seen them live more times than I can count but still think of that first night whenever I hear them.

The gig was a blur, I loved every second. At that time the Charlotte would have been known as one of those venues on the 'toilet circuit'. It was small, a bit rough around the edges and the kind of place where you could feel the bass vibrate through your entire body. Endless crowd-surfers and cheap warm pints were thrown over my head and at one point I remember being part of a hot sweaty throng of fans jumping so closely together that my feet didn't touch the ground for a whole song. I had never experienced anything like it and immediately knew I would come back again and again just to feel this feeling. Every so often I caught sight of you, enraptured, totally in the moment. I think I knew then that you were different. That night you made me a live music addict.

After the gig we lingered behind so that we could thank the band, delighted to see us they added us to the guest list for the next night in Nottingham too – but that is a whole other story for a whole other time.

As we walked home, we didn't stop talking. Embarrassed I admitted to you that even though I had always loved music more than anything else, that had been my first gig – rural west Wales wasn't top of the list on most touring schedules.

I expected you to make fun of me, to decide I wasn't really the sort of girl you wanted to hang around with after all, but the exact opposite happened. You decided that this, our fresher's year, would be the year that you taught me all about this exciting new world. The Charlotte became our second home and while I don't think anything ever topped that first night, we saw so many bands, met so many people and sang until we were hoarse. Those memories got me through a lot, although without you I was never able to set foot in the Charlotte again.

On the nights when the Charlotte was closed, we visited other famous Leicester night spots, two of the best being Mosquito Coast and The Fan Club. One of the worst being Krystal's, although with enough alcohol even that could be fun. When we wanted a more sophisticated night, we would visit The Bank where we once met the then Leicester city goalkeeper Kasey Keller.

Jake and I wander further into the city and find the High Cross shopping centre, unrecognisable to me. I remember this as The Shires, the place that took quite a chunk of my student loan. Every month, on a Thursday afternoon, my friends and I would walk into town and treat ourselves to lunch at Bella Italia before wandering round the shops and treating ourselves to a new top or two. The afternoon always ended with a trip to Deli France for an obligatory cake and cuppa, always a custard filled croissant and mug of steaming hot coffee, we all thought we were so grown up.

Afterwards, when my friends went home I would come and meet you from your part-time job at the Virgin Megastore. There was always some new release you had to share with me as soon as we got back to yours. We would talk about the lyrics, what we thought they meant to the band, what they meant to us. Sometimes I stayed, falling asleep on your bed as you caught up with some late-night radio while finishing your latest assignment. If I'd have known then how limited our time together was, I would never have slept. I would have listened to every song with you, asked what you thought about every single thing and taken in every smile, every laugh and every shared moment between us. There is so much I must have forgotten, so much that was taken for granted, I thought we had forever.

Suddenly I feel cold and as I look around I realise how different things are now. How all the things I came here for are long gone and will never come back. How different my life is from the plans I had made. The sadness takes my breath away.

"I want to go home now," I say.

As we walk back to the car, I catch Jake watching me out of the corner of his eye.

"You clearly loved it here," he says. "Why haven't you come back sooner? We could visit more often. We could stay for a few days. Create some special moments of our own."

I shake my head and think about trying to explain. Where do I even begin without making Jake feel like he is second best? It's not just Leicester I love, it's the memories, it's you. You brought it alive for me. And today, for a brief moment, it brought you back to me. You were there, everywhere I looked and that would never be fair on Jake.

SARAH KIRBY
ST STEPHENS ROAD

IONA MANDAL

Named after the Hebridean island, her name is synonymous with a violet flower in Greek. Born in India, raised in England, studying at King Edward VI Camp Hill Girls, Birmingham. She's a member of the British Mensa High IQ Society and enjoys writing poetry, rock climbing and playing the clarinet.

THE LEICESTER SEAMSTRESS

The Leicester seamstress looks down
at her blank linen.
It is parched and almost too white
for her pupils to bear.
Like a celestial silkworm,
the thread dazzles between her fingers.

She weaves the Golden Mile in a single stroke.
Cross stitches for the people,
she embeds their souls
in dots across the linen.
Some are clustered,
others sequestered.

The thread has no colour this time,
like Joseph's coat,
her masterpiece is woven
with familiar, yet unrecognisable colours
of her own creation.

Chain stitch for the roads,
broken between each cobble,
dust gathers, yet, swept away
by stumbling feet.

Back stitch for pubs,
morphing to curry restaurants,
catering to the evolution of taste buds.

Blanket stitch,
to rest the unhemmed
and always unfinished
edge of the city.

She feels like God.
Six days of work,
and on the seventh,
she hangs her tapestry.

KATHLEEN BELL
Is a writer of poetry and fiction and co-editor of the anthology Over Land,
Over Sea: poems for those seeking refuge. *She is an Associate Professor of
Creative Writing at De Montfort University.*

ABSENCES

He must have rounded the corner from Holy Bones, but I didn't see him. I was
too intent on the brickwork. His voice interrupted my thoughts.

"Roman bricks, those are."

I nodded, couldn't be bothered to turn. I've no need of a man to tell me
what I already know. The voice went on.

"Knocked down half the walls, they did, when the invader left, and good
luck to them. Families made dwellings from those bricks. Generations lived
there. Then came the Norman yoke, and we're still not free of it."

He would not be quiet. So I turned to face him. Looked. A lined face,
though he was not old. Shaggy hair – brown. Baggy shirt – beige, if it was any
colour. Loose trousers, off-black, ending high above his ankles. Tramp, I
thought. Well-informed. Some are, I know, though few stop to hear them. I
sighed. He deserved attention and politeness.

"It's a fine church," I said.

He turned aside and muttered something. I couldn't make out the words.
If I'd had to guess, I'd have thought 'Babylonish steeplehouse' – but that's me
putting a gloss on it. Then he looked back, as though he saw me for the first
time.

"You lost someone," he said. "You've come looking for the dead."
It was a chilly day. I tried to control my face.

"I know," he said. "If it weren't so, you wouldn't see me. You do see me,
don't you?"
I nodded, then looked away at the great height of the Roman wall behind him.

"They often come here," he said. "The lost, I mean. The people who lost
them come too. It should be right – past and present together – but they never
meet. Leastways, I've seen none that did. Who did you lose?"

I wouldn't tell him. Some facts are hard to say. Instead I walked to the
rail and looked over, intent on all that was left of the Roman baths.
He went on and ignored my rudeness.

"I come for my wife and child. Sarah and little Solomon. I know they're gone. The neighbours got word to me. But no-one knew who buried them or if their corpses were left in a heap and burned in one of the fires."

I looked back, tried to catch his eyes but his gaze was fixed on something far away.

"In the siege, it was. After the siege. They hungered and thirsted like the rest, and all the while that heathen Rupert waited with his guns, took counsel with his familiar – the shade of that white dog. He took it everywhere, even into war. The troops of king and pope caroused while those inside the city starved and prayed. The people of Leicester would not give in. They knew what was right. But the king's men came. Some say it was treason by one within, but I think it was Satan came to their aid. It was work of a demon they did. Who did they think was in the city? Half the men were off to war, but the women and children wouldn't give in – not even when Rupert's men broke through the walls with canon and shot.

"That's what they told me. That's what the message said. I'd left Sarah nothing, not even an old musket – just a pair of kitchen knives to guard her honour and the child. Not enough against a gang of drunken soldiers. And that prince, that king –" he turned and spat "– he didn't just *let* the soldiers rampage. He urged them on – told them to take what loot they could from the houses, let them use the women – "

He paused. I thought there might be tears in his eyes, but I looked closely and there were none. His face was calm enough. All the anger was in his voice.

"The women used what weapons they had for defence. The children hurled what they could find – bricks, stones, mud. Nothing stopped the king's men. Nothing. Three days they rioted and ransacked. They took everything. Then they stopped. The town was bruised and battered but it watched them go. People put out the little fires and set to work. Rebuilding – that's what good folk do. Each who lived went back to his own place. Neighbours took in those whose homes were destroyed. They sought the dead and buried them – some here in this churchyard, others – where they were allowed. But no-one saw Sarah again. No-one knew what became of little Solomon."

"Perhaps they escaped," I suggested, though I didn't know what comfort that might be.

He went on as though he hadn't heard.

"The last time Sarah was seen she had a great sword-slash to her brow and our little one was limp, slung over one shoulder. She had a ladle in her hand – a ladle – and she chased a soldier down a street and into an alley. After that, nothing. They said the wound was bad. They didn't know how she could stand or run, or if she was already dead and walking. I won't see them here – not ever. But I have to come back. I have to believe it could happen.

"I did my best for them. I was in the Protector's army, fighting for God and the right. Just after I heard the news we were at Naseby, all lined up with pikes, ready to make God's kingdom here on earth. I tried to fight for God, but it was vengeance I desired. I thought that every time I dragged my pike and the soul from a man's guts, I'd lose a bit of the hurt from what they'd done to Sarah, and what they might have done to my son. But it wasn't like that. With each thrust the grief grew heavier and, in the end, I was pushing and thrusting and dragging the way I'd been taught with tears running down my cheeks and nothing in my head but my sweet Sarah, my darling Solomon, and how what we had together was nothing like this war and this world – nothing at all. And joy departed from me forever, though I prayed to God and tried to live a good, Christian life."

He faced me.

"And your grief," he said, "is it as great as this?"

I couldn't speak – just looked at him.

"For you it will not pass," he said, "but the burden will lessen. You will learn to carry it with you and be thankful for its weight. Come, let us walk together – just a little way."

So, I walked with him on the outskirts of old Leicester, over the canal, past the dismantled railway, through the spot where the Bowstring Bridge had been – all things that had been made and fallen into disuse or destroyed since his time.

At last I turned towards the new university buildings, the ones that rose over the Roman spoil-heaps, the mediaeval streets and the siege-wall foundations. There he turned aside.

"That's where the killing was," he said, and gestured.

"Sometimes I hear the screams, though I never did in life. Be thankful you cannot hear them – that those sounds are not in your ear."

I watched him walk through Bede Park towards the Narborough Road: a tramp, you would have said, a man of no account – though perhaps you wouldn't have seen him at all. Then I walked to where the siege walls had been, and he was right. I could hear no screaming.

Around me the living chattered. A young woman laughed, and somewhere in the distance a blackbird sang.

MACK MATHOD

Is an artist, educator, dramatist, writer, comedian, a Mack of all trades. He was born in Leicester in 1950 before going to Leeds College of Art and London where he worked in scriptwriting and education until his retirement. Mack is now catching up on forgotten ambitions before it is too late!

BOOMER

The time has now arrived. It is now 2019 and us Baby Boomers are ready to tell it all. Consequently, as I was born in January of 1950 it is my responsibility to tell you a story from my generation. A generation starting with a ration book and ending with a Facebook.

This is my story of everything, or, at least all that I can remember. It has been an interesting time where I have been thrown in to the bubbling river of change many times and have managed to avoid drowning, even to clamber onto the shoreline occasionally to take in the sights. Where to start, sorry, yes, I'll make a start. Where? The beginning? No, no, as any artist will tell you, and, as I constantly tell my students now, always paint the background first. Then you can paint over your unwanted bits later.

The background was Leicester just after the war. My mum and dad had had two children, a boy, Donald and later a girl: Olive, then, like the rest of the world, time stopped, and the War took over their lives. My dad never talked about his wartime life, probably not because it was too awful to mention but more that he survived it all and that was enough. Judging by the sepia photos of smiling uniformed soldiers in decorated rickshaws and pyramid backdrops he was in North Africa with Monty, I suppose. Our lives were never close enough to give him the opportunity for him to speak of it all. It wasn't important, in fact; I imagine he would have thought that the story was not worth telling. There must have been many like him, not Colditz, Normandy or Berlin just survival. He occasionally mentioned Tobruk and Bengasi to illustrate our pampered fifties lifestyle but that was all. That was enough for me as, when he returned to his little terraced house in Leicester, things had to move on. As my mum put it so succinctly "He came back from the War and started all his funny business again". The 'Funny Business' she was referring to resulted in the birth of a daughter, Freda and, seventeen months later the Baby Boomer himself… me.

Like most boomers I was born at home, in the upstairs front room of 47, Bardolph Street, Leicester. At the time my Dad had a job as a porter for the LMS Railway and Mum was a nurse. I should imagine that at the time they were both fairly contented with their lot; house, job, healthy kids and, although there was not much money around, the mood was a wartime leftover of make-do-and-mend and we made do with a lot. The wages from nursing and portering was not much and we accepted second best a lot. In a terraced house in a terraced street the horizon was as far as you could see and that was the end of the next terrace. I know, I know, I'm going to come up with "but we were happy" but happiness is only a comparative concept and to a small three-year-old the issue did not occur.

At three the only issue that I remember occurring was the gross injustice of Coronation Day 1953. It was a time when it seemed like everyone was in agreement, but then that was a child's point of view. Certainly, in the terraced backstreets of Leicester the Coronation was an excuse to join together and celebrate something. Nowadays with the dissipation of religious belief, a more questioning approach to the monarchy and a deluge of other entertainment, a Coronation would be a contentious division of allegiances but in 1953 it seemed all of England, certainly all of the terraced streets of Leicester, had something to cheer about. I remember every window had a display, either homemade or cut out of the *Daily Express*, of the Queen and Prince Philip.

Every top window had a string of bunting or a Union Jack wedged under the sill so that it protruded into the street. One of my earliest memories of the haves and the have nots is that working people in terraces all had flags either left over from the war or homemade whereas, if you walked out of the terraces and into the wealthy semi-detached of Doncaster Road and beyond you would see proper flagpoles flying, not cheap or faded flags but brand spanking new Union Jacks with twiddly gold knobs on the ends. It was my first experience that some people had better things than I had. However, that was not the injustice of the day. The bunting was hung across the street and everyone's dining table was brought out into the street for a street party.

I remember the flags, the tables and the dressing up very well. Everyone wore their Sunday clothes and the children, Boomer included, were dressed up as fairy tale characters to take part in a procession from the corrugated assembly Hall at the end of the street around the tables and back. Freda was in her prettiest dress and a homemade bonnet and looked resplendent with decorated garden cane as Bo Peep. Boomer, for some reason, was elected to be Mary,

Mary Quite Contrary, probably because Mum had no other clothes for me, and the 'contrary' part fitted me like a glove. Unfortunately, when the judges put us into boys' and girls' groups, I was mistakenly put into the girl's group, an insignificant act in itself but a source of hilarity over the next fifty years when Christmas time family anecdotes are exchanged in front of newcomers. It would not have been an astute observation to say that that one judge's tiny mistake had a profound influence on my personality and sexual identity later in life and that because of that understandable misjudgment I have held a grudge against gender stereotypes to this day, but it didn't, and I haven't. The only regret was that, like with many such occasions, Dad's box camera appeared and captured the moment for posterity... infinite posterity.

I remember those early days of hope with a fondness that I can still resurrect now. It was a time when things were new and there was a freshness in the atmosphere of England that even a small boy could feel. My dad was impressed with the Festival of Britain and even I can remember the space age innovation that was the Skylon. He had a hope for the future that was more informed by Dan Dare than political solution. One day we would all live a better life and Dad wanted to take us there but, like the Festival, it was not for the likes of us and, more importantly, it was out of our price range. Instead we could only gaze at the marvels in the *Daily Mirror* like children with our noses pressed against an expensive toy shop window.

By now, Dad had changed his job and had a better paid one delivery driving for the Co-operative Society. Like the Railways, the Co-op was held highly amongst the working class. It was their shop, they owned it and once a year it would pay out a dividend to all its customers.

Many families like us depended on that 'Divi' to give us a Christmas or school clothes or holiday kit. So, dad working for the Co-op was a step up. Unfortunately, Mum's situation was not as good. She had more or less given up full time nursing to look after her two new children and with Donald and Olive still at home the house was full. Her legs, not always good at the best of times, were paying the price for the years of nursing and now she was suffering from chronic osteoarthritis which made her legs take on water and cause her to be almost entirely housebound. She loved her family even if the older ones were straining at the leash to escape. Donald had had a poor time at school, more a practical boy than academic, he had run away from home once and he looked forward to getting away. On the other hand, Olive was an artist, very creative and needed to be at Art college.

The time, however, was wrong, college cost money and good practical training was only available in the army. Luckily the National Service saved Donald from a wayward track and gave him a direction he otherwise would not have had. When he came out, he, like his father, joined the LMS railway and for a while was as happy as he had ever been. A practical apprenticeship on the footplate doing the job he had a passion for. Olive, on the other hand, had to make do with the creative world of the hairdressing salon instead of the artist studio and between them they managed to make the most of the inadequate education provision for the working class. The wind of change however was a long way off for Boomer. I went to school and took on the school system from the more junior standpoint.

I have always been a watcher. All my life I have watched things happen. I suppose I've never really taken part, just watched. My friends always accused me of being 'over punctual'; something I call 'the Basingstoke Syndrome' *. I suppose it's a disease, a disease some of us have by being over obsessed with time. We are never late; in fact, we are always far too early to be of any use. I have spent long hours of my life waiting for events to happen; trains to arrive, shows to start, appointments to meet. I have never been late for anything in my life allowing me to ponder, to afford the waiting time to watch people in the comfort of my own mind. It is the observing rather than the doing that makes it all so interesting. The majority of us, no matter what we might think, are not doers. Only a few manage to play, to compete, to perform and even then, most of the players don't come first and have to watch the backside of the winners go on and win. The rest of us don't even get that close; we just watch.

My earliest memory is of watching my mother watching me. I would catch her out of the corner of my eye, or from a mirror or a reflection from the teapot that was always the well-worshiped centrepiece of our kitchen table. We seemed to live and survive on tea and, through that brown earthenware shine, I would catch my mother watching my every movement. Her tired brown eyes filled with love, a deep, gnawing love that would take me forty years to experience. A love that would give me everything without question, would understand my every anger, appreciate my every frustration and forgive my every youthful narrowness.

I also would watch painfully as my father and mother's marriage deteriorated until they both were clinging on to a relationship so wafer thin, we all feared by even mentioning it that it would crumble into dust. My father, a proud and bitter man who had survived two wars thought he could have done much more with his life than the unfair cards he had been dealt.

Although he spent most of his peace behind a steering wheel, he was no van driver and no union man but his belief in the socialism of the Co-op was rivalled only by his love of the Railway. Just as his strong belief in the Primitive Methodist church was matched by his impeccable Sunday appearance and his upright demeanour. Contrast his sad frustrated ambition with my mother's acceptance of whatever was thrown at her. If his was the role of the misunderstood and incomplete, hers was the opposite. The lot she had been given was to care for others and she did care. In her early days as a district nurse she cared for and was cared about by many. My childhood memory of being woken by a midnight door knock, which would mean another difficult labour or another fever to care for, was a vivid one.

Later when her chronic arthritis would blow here legs into tree trunks and I would watch as she bandaged them with long canvas strips like a soldier winding on his puttees, she would tell me nostalgically of her nursing episodes. She had once been beautiful, and the caring had taken its toll, but she would not complain, especially to a fidgeting careless listener who could only watch as the pain disfigured her and slowly rotted away the life from her soul. Eventually it would even try her patience with a small boy who wanted to be Superman...
I very quickly came to the conclusion that I was not Superman, and neither was anyone else.

The Stafford family lived on the other side of the street and me and Tony Stafford were the best of friends, although I had the distinct feeling even then that the Stafford's were even lower working class than us. Seared in my memory was a trip to the circus with the Stafford's. Because I was invited late, we were a ticket short and Mrs Stafford got me through the turnstile by insisting that I had lost my ticket. It shocked me to the core that a grown woman could blatantly lie. My first circus experience was ruined by the thought that I had gained admittance by false pretense. It was my first experience of a lie and it stayed with me for the rest of my life.

Tony and I spent most of our time together in the street, making dirt roadways in his back yard or sitting on the pavement observing the minutia of the earth. This usually involved research into the ant and caterpillar population of the street. How many of the former could be stamped on and what colour were the gooey insides of the latter when burnt under a magnifying glass. It was during one of the more devastating ant culls with bodies piling up high around the nest under Mrs. Bramble's front step that one of those life-changing observations happened. I looked up and, turning the corner into the street, walked a young man wearing a smart black jacket and open necked shirt who was almost at a sprint in his haste. He was weeping big heavy sobs and holding his face where blood soaked his white handkerchief and splashed onto his white shirt. He stumbled on without realising his presence was searing into a young boy's memory and would sit there forever. Tony, I remember, never looked up from the ant holocaust, and seconds later the man was gone but he lives on with me still, my first sight of blood, my first sight of violence, but, more than the bloody violence, was the first terrible sight a man's tears.

*The Basingstoke Syndrome was coined from when the family went on our holidays to Bournemouth. The train would stop at Basingstoke in order to change engines and my Dad would take the opportunity to get out of our compartment to get teas from the station buffet. This terrified me, fearing the train would leave without him and so make me fatherless. A paranoia that has forever stayed with me and making me a slave to punctuality for the rest of my life

CALKE ABBEY
COLONIAL COUNTRYSIDE

Here we have some writing from our future. A local Leicester primary school took part in University of Leicester's Colonial Countryside project investigating colonial links to National Trust properties in the UK. These extracts are from work on Calke Abbey, a property on the Leicestershire Derbyshire border. Colonial Countryside is a child-led writing and history project about National Trust houses' Caribbean and East India Company connections. Steered by a child advisory board, this five year project has assembled authors, historians and primary pupils to commission, resource and publish new writing. 100 primary children will visit 10 National Trust properties and craft new writing, presenting it to live, print and digital audiences.

Calke Abbey shows that empire shaped upper-class domestic settings. As Colonial Countryside historian Sarah Longair states, objects such as tiger skins remind us tiger hunting was a major feature of colonial life in India. The tiger symbolised India, and a tiger skin represented the domination of the colonised nation. In Calke's library there is an 1840s atlas which shows 'British possessions in North America', indicating how we used to think of colonies elsewhere. The library also contains a globe from 1870, showing the red lines of empire which were set to advance further in the years to come. Sarah Longair points out that the demand for luxury goods, such as the Chinese bed hangings at Calke, also tell us a great deal about the commercial driving force behind the rise of the East India Company. The exotic wood coromandel table upstairs tells a different story, about the environmental destruction wrought by empire. The Tibetan skull cup is a fascinating item too. Displayed in a cabinet of curiosities, the skull was once a sacred item – hewn from a human skull following a sky burial, where birds picked clean the corpses and the skull was retrieved as a way of remembering human mortality. The item – nestling among seeds, a mosque tile and other artefacts – tells us a lot about how colonial-era objects were displayed. Today, as the children have pointed out, it raises issues about objects being taken out of context.
There are also ethical questions. As one child put it: 'what if that skull belonged to my mother or grandmother?'

MICHELLE
THE SKULL CUP

I see something in a case, a glass case – something round, something bumpy,
something I've never seen before.
It looks plastic or maybe metal. I wonder what it is, so I walk closer.
It isn't plastic. It isn't metal. It is bone. A skull. A human skull from a sky
burial in Tibet, picked clean. Picked fresh.
People drank out of it to remember the dead, to remember they too will die.
I wondered how I would feel if it was my mother's or father's skull. Would I
care for it? Would I use it? Would it be covered with leaves, letters and rocks
too?

AMMAAR
TIGERSKIN

People from England took over different countries,
tracking tigers to use as rugs.
They kill them, take their skins and fur,
Sell them. Only thinking about money.
They will have holes in them. Killed by rifles.
Sniping cats,
taking those poor tigers' lives away,
using them as soulless servants
& keeping them to show off to posh visitors.

MAI
MAHOGANY

Enslaved Africans taken from their loved ones,
Sent on ships to greedy people.
Poor Africans climbing up giants,
Chopping trees for selfish people.
Tortured Africans carrying heavy trees off to sea, to ships,
Suffering miseries that weren't for them.

DANIEL
MAHOGANY FURNITURE

Old slaves climbing colossal trees
Ragged clothes, pinched faces.
Sawing the trees angrily
to make vivid mahogany
furniture
for rich people.
Men and children transported from their continent.

Whacking the trees with axes,
the slaves not enjoying themselves.
They don't want to do this,
eating bad meals for dinner.
Not being winners.

ETHAN
THE BED

Isolated. In a dark, cold, pitch black room, all by itself. Unused.
Never used.
Bought just for show.
I take a step further. I see an elegant bed.
My eyes lock on the kaleidoscope of bright colours.
Nowadays, this bed is the most elegant in Leicester. The oldest in Leicester.
The bed looks more like a Chinese temple. So many animals printed on the
curtains.

MAI
I SAW A PRINCESS BED

I saw a princess type bed. Stranded in a dark and quiet room.
At first, I was really jealous, but when I discovered more, I was disgusted. Why
was it in a dark room?
The bed had many features like blossoms, tigers, flowers and much more.
But one thing hooked on me, the fact that there was a house with people in it,
but as my eyes zoomed across the curtains, I saw a story. A love story.
A man fighting for a girl.
The bed itself was an emblem of fortune.
Questions raced against my head. But no one knew the full story behind it.

As I looked around I saw something, something that made me curious, that said
the bed couldn't get too hot and didn't want to be in a bright light.
I wouldn't really want to sleep in that bed after I heard that slaves
Children and men had made the bed in darkness just to make the rich happy.
When I looked carefully it made me think what did it look to me?
It was a question that couldn't be answered.
But it was like paradise.

SIMAKADA
A GLOBE IN A LIBRARY

A globe in a library a globe lined with longitude and latitude.
Spinning spinning spinning away taking knowledge from all of a Japanese sea
and green grass moving spirally.
A colour line countries whatever it means.
A ball of knowledge for you and me.
The whole world in a library what a wonderful feeling it is quite a useful object
and a special opportunity.

TAQIABBAS
THE TIGER RUG

Someone just shot a tiger
His heart is filled with fire
What did the tiger do?
He's just walking around
Not going after you
Why did you kill it?
Just to make a rug
Just use your life
A little hard work
Use your time very positively
You don't have to be extremely cruel
Have happiness, dignity with no gun
Just because you're very rich
You don't have the right
To kill and ruthlessly fight
This is what the colonial masters used to do
In India. Oh they are annoying and violent
Horribly violent!

NICOLA HUMPHREYS

Is a part-time writer with a full-time job to pay the bills. She writes under the name 'A Rambling Collective' on her blog and Twitter. Enjoys "making stuff up" about people who exist inside her own head and lives with her Yorkshireman boyfriend. All of her dresses have pockets.

MAY SETTLE IN TRANSIT

"I don't think we should have owt for dinner. We'll just make do." Mark says, pointing at the huge slices of millionaire shortbread and lemon drizzle on the table in front of us.

"Remember we're having an early curry tonight before the gig. We'll be pogged. I'm right looking forward to it."

We're sat in a coffee shop that used to be a posh jeweller, that used to be a bridal store. I'm still a little shocked that everything is so different to how I remember it round here. Like Fenwicks. I loved that shop, with its creaky rabbit warren staircases. I imagined how there would have been an uproar in the Mercury when it was closing. The menu in the English restaurant across the road hasn't altered much over the years. Mark used to go there all the time for "proper canteen school dinners", whenever he was sick of pretending to like my veggie meals, or when he missed his mam's cooking. He's of the 'ain't broke, don't' fix it' school. To find a restaurant anywhere that's full every lunchtime with people wanting home cooked food is good going these days.

"Mum? Look at this."

Charlie hands me her phone and I press the little triangle in the middle of the screen. Within five seconds I'm watching a YouTube video of the old council buildings being demolished. I instinctively put my hand briefly over my mouth, then say,

"Gosh, wow! That's amazing. They were horrible though. It was virtually a wind tunnel walking between them."

I press the screen to watch it again.

"I'm glad New Walk is still like it was. You know I must have walked down there a thousand times. Even that 60s concrete building fits right in. Your dad used to skateboard down there, and this one time, this man shouted, 'this is for pedestrians' at him, so he shouted back 'it doesn't say no skateboarding on the sign.' Then, when the man shouted, 'bloody students' at him, your dad circled back, briefly paused and did that chest thump black power fist sign in front of him."

I sigh deeply.

"I still can't believe that we've only walked about half a mile from the station and so much has changed. A sign of the times, I suppose. "

"Mum, are you going all resentrification again?"

"No, I didn't mean that at all. Ask your Dad, Charl. He's a designer so can explain it better." I say.

"It's not that I'm against progress, love." Mark says,

"It's just that it will take a lot more than luxury apartments and offices, above supermarket express and noodle bar, to reinvent our urban landscapes. If we want to build a proper community where we live, then we ave to provide spaces, and that costs money. You know, give students and young professionals an incentive to settle here after they've finished their studies. You know what I mean, love. Just look what they did to the libraries and our swimming pools and even the prisons. It's always about the bottom line with that lot. Tha don't think on"

He rubs his fingers together, the universal money gesture.

"Ma mate was telling me about the regeneration of that place over there, near the river down the road, and company he works for had put in a bid, for housing and schools, doctors an all that, but it was rejected, cos returns for the shareholders would take nine years, and that was considered to be too long. Too long! I reckon nine years is not too long for a brand new society to bed in, grow and evolve from scratch. We had our industrial revolution, then lost our manufacturing industry abroad and now investors are renting out the same warehouses and factories to rich students from those countries making brass from our industry. Anyroad, love, I'll wind me neck in and stop chelpin. We didn't bring you here today to give you a lesson in capitalism. You'll get that at college. This is your day love."

We sit for a minute in that contemplative silence you get when you are truly comfortable in someone else's company and space. Mark stirs the tea then pours a cup of the hot, amber liquid.

"And they know how to make a proper brew in here. They even warm cup up beforehand." Mark says.

Charlie fiddles with her phone. She takes a picture of me, as I pause, hand cradling the turquoise cup, poised to sip my perfect coffee.

"Didn't you get in at Salford as well, mum?" she asks.

"Yeah I did, and Keele, and it was really hard to decide where to go. D'you know, in my first term here, I thought I'd made a mistake cos I was so homesick and crying all the time. I hadn't even moved a hundred miles away and I felt stuck. Your grandma said I should give it a bit longer to try and get used to it. She said that there were a lot of people who'd lost everything and had no choice but to come here, and from a lot further away than I had, so if they could make Leicester their home forever, then I could do it for three years. So I was going to think about it over the Christmas holidays, but then I met your Dad."

I reach for Mark's hand and he squeezes mine, then he strokes the back of my hand with his thumb. I know she's taking our photograph. She's always taking photographs. She's often invisible, but quick, as she captures private moments.

"What you doing now, nebbin?"
asks Mark incredulously as Charlie starts typing into her phone. A moment later she shows holds her arm out to show us the screen. There's a photograph of us two gazing at each other, from thirty seconds ago with:

'Find someone who looks at you like how my Mum and Dad look at each other 🖤 soppy' typed underneath.

Mark rolls his eyes, shakes his head and tuts. Then he smiles and looks down. A moment later he's blowing his nose, then wiping his eyes and cleaning his glasses. Charlie and I smile at each other. We're all a bit misty-eyed today. It's a big deal coming back.
After a few seconds, Mark puts his arm round me and gives my upper arm a firm, reassuring, jiggly squeeze, then releases his grip. I sniff, wipe my nose with the back of my hand, reach for my cup, and continue.

"I wanted to be closer to London, but not actually move properly down south. It would have been too much too soon. I wanted somewhere where there would be loads of food I could eat. Hummus and moussaka get really boring. And the sewing thing. It seemed a bit pointless to move back home every summer to get a job, and lose my flat. I may as well stay here and work. Anyway, I couldn't work in that garlic bread factory back home again. I was like a skunk. The smell just would not go. But that one summer when all I did was sew children's tracksuits for three months was probably just as boring. Did my head it so much that I used to dream about them."

"Remember when you made Simon's football team some trackkies when they went to France?" asks Charlie.

"So I did. Gosh, Charl, you've got a good memory. I'd totally forgotten about that."

"They loved those little tracksuits. They were so proud wearing them. I even embroidered their initials onto the tops like professional footballers have. I made twenty sets so they'd have spares, not just for those that were in the team."

"Ten percent contingency."

Charlie and Mark both say in unison.

"What about you Dad? Why d'you pick Loughborough?"

"It had the best engineering course love, and I thought they were bound to have a decent running club what with it being sports college an all."

I remember myself being a lean and smooth skinned student like the ones I see walking around me today, but their mashup of eras in clothing confuses me. I have to remind myself that the 80s are new to them. Charlie's even wearing Doc Martens and ripped jeans today, except our jeans were torn through wear not fashion.

It's a bit overwhelming that our baby girl is thinking about University. Footwear Design plus Economics and Mandarin. She's our daughter all right. Time used to be measured in candles on a cake or pencil marks on the door frame. Now, she's taller than me and I was never that confident.

Before the internet, everyone had address books filled with our friends' parents' details so we could keep in touch. Going home for Christmas meant a couple of handwritten letters, and the odd postcard from abroad. Now I have friends I chat to on Twitter every week, but I know I'll never meet them or maybe never even know their real name.

We used to walk down to Filbert Street and buy a ticket on the gate or even decide to see a band on the spur of the moment. People hitchhiked or went interrailing around Europe. There was a loose arrangement between everyone we knew who followed bands, to meet up at the Glastonbury Festival every year on Saturday at 2 o'clock, just like the song said. You knew there'd always be someone there you'd met before, from a gig, or whose floor you'd slept on.

Not anymore. I doubt you've been able to do that for a long time. I think they've known the name address, date of birth and photograph of virtually everyone who buys a ticket for Glastonbury for several years now. Our glory years are ITV3, ticket stubs and letters in a floral box under the bed.

My most vivid memories of my youth are as tangible as the projections in the Richard III museum. It's hard not to feel like a tourist watching my old life. Were people really kinder to each other back then or am I just being naive?

She likes it here. I want to take her to all the University cities on her list, so she's not dazzled or disappointed when she decides which one to go to, if any. She's got so much more to lose than we did. It'll take her until she's our age to pay it all back, whatever she decides.

"Those lanes are beautiful.",

"I haven't seen a chain store yet.",

"It's almost a little Chinatown here",

"These cobbles are so pretty",

"Did a pie shop really invent crisps?",

"I can't believe his body was so close to the surface all that time and remained intact.",

"Is this building really six hundred years old?"

Opening a prison cell door window in the Guildhall, she depresses the brass light button to illuminate the tiny room, and then peers inside. She is a little startled seeing the mannequins, dressed as they would have been, except they look and smell a lot cleaner. I think she can no more relate to how different our lives were in this city twenty odd years ago, than she can to how theirs were hundreds of years ago.

Graffiti tags are now sanitized commissioned artworks. Murals of local pride. The damp, dripping underpasses that used to be avoided after dark, have become clean public squares with light installations in the disabled-friendly flooring. Dodgy pubs are now themed bars, with in-house mixologists specialising in gin cocktails, which sit seamlessly alongside micro brewed bespoke ales and burgers at fifteen quid a pop. New steakhouses with grandiose, original features from former banks.

Mark was right. Those disused shoe and sock factories had been transformed into purpose-built student flats with rents per room more than the cost of our mortgage. We'd seen that retro-industrial phase in buildings - the visible air ducts instead of ceilings, exposed pipes and bricks, unfinished paintwork, vintage telephone or photo booths, concrete floors and pull chains in the loos - gradually creep further north over the last few years so why was I so unprepared to see it here?

Mark comes out of the sweet shop with "a quarter of spice" and offers us the open paper bag. I take out a rhubarb and custard and hold it between my index finger and thumb. Needing a moment to compose myself, I put the back of my hand over my mouth, press my tongue to the roof of my mouth to try and stop myself sobbing again, close my eyes, then breathe in deeply and hold my breath.

"You all right love?"

Mark asks gently, and then hugs me again. Charlie roots around in her backpack and hands me a tissue.

"Thanks Charl." I say, sniffing again. "I don't know what's wrong with me today. Memories I suppose. Probably my hormones."

"You always think of a place that you love as staying the same when you've gone. And even though you know that your old life is over, and you might never see this folk again, you're never quite ready to let go."

"Dad, that's beautiful." Charlie says.

I overhear snippets of conversation as we pass a group of potential students on the same open day walking trail.

"Just yer bog-standard en-suite,"

and

"I thought about applying for one of those studios with the underfloor heating and security cameras, but it was £175 a week. Anyway, they'd all gone. You get your own washer dryer and flat screen, you know."

All this was a far cry from my grotty flat above a shop up London Road. It wasn't as bad as I'm making it out to be, because my course-mate Sonia and I, lived there for two years, then Mark and I for another year after that while I did my PGCE. It wasn't damp or cold and I felt safe. There was a phone, and the landlord put in an electric shower and deadbolt once he saw how serious we were about staying. He came around after two months to check up on the flat, and he could not hold in his delight that we'd painted the rooms, got lampshades, a washing machine, new curtains and put some rugs down. It was always spotless and none of us smoked. I remember buying so much fabric from one of the shops on Belgrave Road that I had to get a taxi back. I spent all week making curtains with blackout linings to block out the street light, and loose covers for the sagging sofa, but it was worth it. I made it into a home.

"Mum, will you take me to that pub, where you met?" she asks.

"I think it's near here actually. Look, it's opposite that."

I say, pointing to a medieval building on her phone.

"What's a Magazine?" she asks.

"I think it was a gateway to the walled bit of the city about 600 years ago." I say.

"They probably stored weapons in it as well at some point."

We walk down one-way streets with wide pavements and then we spot someone we recognise. We've never actually spoken to him before, but it's definitely him. He was known as the 'man who looks at sky'. Always alone, head held high, chin raised. Face turned up, peering down his nose. A tall man with a half-empty backpack, anorak, hiking boots. I imagined he couldn't possibly see where he was going. I wondered if he had walked this route every day for the last twenty odd years. His life was his very own Groundhog Day or Trueman Show.

As we turn the corner, my heart remembers. The old sign is still there but it's no longer a pub. It's an Oriental Supermarket now.

"Tell me how you met again, Mum?"

"You know that church that Grandma goes to? Well, there's a map in the foyer so you can stick a pin in the city where your kid goes to University. Your Uncle Dave's parents went to the same church so they arranged for us to meet up so he could take me to the local church. That was their plan, anyway. In reality, Dave was actually showing me and my friend June round the local nightlife, and the third time we all went out, his friends came too. We went to see 'The Fall' in this very pub. Your dad and his mate were staying at Dave's cos they couldn't get back to Loughborough. Those three were right little globetrotters. They used to go all over in Dave's campervan, following bands, picking up hitchers and sleeping in it after gigs when they could get away with it"

"Yer mam made us some curtains for the van so you couldn't see inside, and cushion covers an everything. We were very lucky. Only once did police knock on window and tell us to move on. He breathalysed Dave first though to check." says Mark.

"There want much CCTV back then. You wouldn't be able to do it now love. You'd get a fixed penalty or moved on for rough sleeping or summat. It'd probably be cheaper to get Travelodge anyroad."

"I think we did go to his church once, when his Mum and Dad came down when they took us all out for Sunday lunch."

"Stand where you had your first kiss, Mum." Charlie says.

The man behind the counter looks up from his book and exchanges a bemused look with Mark, but they say nothing. I think it's the secret Dad code of 'if in doubt, say nowt'. I wonder if the shopkeeper gets visitors reminiscing in here all of the time. Charlie notices and feels the need to explain.

"For the 'gram, Dad."

Later on, in the hotel, while Mark is in the shower, and Charlie is sat on the other bed, watching something on her laptop with her headphones on, I scroll through my Instagram. It's full of snapshots and little videos from today. Our old stomping ground afresh through her eyes.

'Checked out Leicester DMU with my parents. Amazing food. #Les-Tah. #curry. #PrincessCharlotte. #wheretheyfirstmet.. ♥

Thirty likes and three comments from people I don't know.

One commenter writes 'Were you named after a pub? 😜'

I double tap the screen so a little red heart appears, then I carry on scrolling through my feed.

STUART HILL

Is the award-winning author of the acclaimed Icemark Trilogy of historical fantasy novels. The Cry of the Icemark was published in 2005 by Chicken House and won the inaugural Waterstones Children's Book Prize. 2013 saw the release of the first prequel to the Icemark series entitled Prince of the Icemark.

GOD'S HUS PRIORY IN MEYNELL'S PARK.

This was written for an artist friend of Stuarts who wanted it as the basis for a graphic novel he was planning. Nothing came of his friend's proposed art-work for one reason and another. This is set in Meynell's Park in Braunstone:

God's Hus Priory was a crumbling memory made of fading stone. Above ground one wall remained, pierced by a high Gothic window and a doorway that had stood forever open since the day, many years before, when the last shred of wood from its wide and mighty doors, had crumbled into dust. The window was glazed with a view of twisted trees; a last stand of the 'Wild Wood' that had grown when the ice sheets had melted. But time and the axe had pared the forest back to what seemed a chance gathering of oak and beech, holly and yew. And now the bones of the priory stood in nothing more than a small, ragged wood besieged by abandoned cars, fridges and bikes.

Just beyond the borders of the straggling trees a housing estate dreamt the dreams of dead architects and made a nightmare of peoples' lives. The first concrete walls had risen when Hitler still only aspired to genocides, but now the wide boulevards were a desolation of broken roads, and wilderness gardens. Children played in dust that hadn't the strength to be allegory and youths sat astride their bikes on corners and smoked or bragged of crimes committed or planned.

Billy Morrison was one such youth; he'd lived on the Estate all his short life. His dad had chosen his name before going away, one of the few things he had from a man he couldn't recall.

Billy had agreed to meet Jim Kershaw, a friend he supposed. He was bringing Kathy Ridge, a girl who was as tough as Doc Martins.

God's Hus Priory, just off the Braunstone Crossroads, was the meeting point; perhaps they'd smoke, drink, do the usual stuff. Billy headed that way on his bike, speeding down Braunstone Lane, standing in the peddles to build up speed, but then sitting back in case anyone saw him and thought he looked too keen.

It was a grey damp day, and the wood dripped quietly as he approached. Night seemed to have already gathered under the trees and he slowed as he scanned the shadows for signs of life. Nothing and no one.

The way in was overarched by twisted trunks and reaching boughs, and as he finally stopped and straddled his bike, a wind moaned, finding a voice in the branches. Billy shivered. He wasn't cold, but he zipped his jacket anyway just in case someone had seen and thought him scared. His tough, life-weary face would've fooled anyone, but not quite himself. The place felt...odd. Odder than usual anyway.

But then he thought he saw a flash of colour deep in the shadows. Jim perhaps, or Kathy. He swept forward into the dark. Now it *was* cold and there was a smell of wet earth and last year's leaves. His tyres hissed through clinging mud and his breath steamed on the air.

He thought of shouting but then didn't. Shouting for someone showed you wanted them, and Billy liked to think he needed no one at all. If he found them, then OK, and if he didn't that was fine too.

The twisted trees began to thin out as he knew they would and soon he reached the clearing where the ruins of God's Hus Priory stood. He stopped and scanned the one remaining wall. It was smothered in graffiti, and someone who thought he was Banksy had painted a giant rat holding a banner. 'Ban the Bun' it read and a mushroom cloud rose over a teacake.

Billy pedalled slowly closer. There was no one else around and he had to decide if he wanted to wait or not.

"You're here then," a voice from the shadows of the doorway.

"I'm here," he agreed and tried to see the face that'd made the words.

"Kathy with you?"

"Na, mate. Sure she's coming?"

"Said she would," Jim Kershaw answered and pedalled his bike into the half light of the clearing.

Billy shrugged. "Got any smokes?"

"Some; not many,"
Jim was mean with his stuff, no matter how much he had there was never enough to share.

Billy grinned.

"Won't need mine then," and he took a pack from his pocket and lit up.

"Mine won't last," Jim whined.

"You'd best be careful with 'em then."

A sudden sweep of colour through the gloom caught their eyes and they stared expecting Kathy, but saw only a bird. A jay, its grey-blue plumage as bright as flame against the shadows.

"What's that?" Jim asked his voice stuffed with dread.

"Just a bird."

"What sort; it didn't look real?"

"How the hell would I know?" said Billy, knowing its species, knowing it was a member of the crow family, loving its wild flaming flight. Admitting nothing.

"It's creepy in here today," said Jim, his eyes darting around the trees.

Billy shrugged and thought it was creepy every day. Creepy and wild and sad and lost and dangerous and exciting. He shrugged again. Said nothing.

"I don't think Kathy's coming."

"Her choice."

"Yeah. What d'you want to do?"

In answer Billy rode through the high gothic door of the priory and into the wide grassy sweep that would once have been its floor. Jim followed, the chain of his bike squeaking monotonously with every revolution of the pedals.

Trees reached over the ruined priory, almost making a roof with their tortured branches, but not quite. Billy looked up and could see the grey, lowering sky, pregnant with rain. "It'll be dark soon," he said.

"Yeah, so?" asked Jim, the sneer in his tone designed to show he wasn't scared of the ruins after nightfall.

"So perhaps there'll be something to see."

"You can't see note in the dark."

Billy smiled. He had an odd smile. His face didn't so much 'light up' as 'dark down'. Shadows gathered in the natural folds of flesh and his eyes became deep, like twin tunnels leading somewhere shadowed and cold.

"They say there's an entrance to an undercroft around here somewhere."

"A what?" asked Jim his voice cracking.

"A cellar, or crypt," Billy explained. "Perhaps we could find it."

"A cellar, of this old church thing?" Jim was sceptical. "Na, it'll have collapsed yonks ago."

"There's no sign of any subsid… any floor sinking. It's still as level as a footy pitch. So whatever's underneath must still be sound; come on let's see if we can find a way in."

He biked slowly across the wide space ignoring Jim's whining protests. "There can't be a way in; and even if there is, no one's ever found it."

Billy remembered an old church he'd visited on a school trip last summer. It'd had a crypt and the entrance had been hidden in a little archway behind the altar. The teacher with them, old Mr Jenkins, was a fat git, but he knew his churches, and Billy had listened as he always did.

He stopped in the middle of the floor and tried to work out where the altar would've been, and realised it must've stood under the one surviving window that faced east.

"Over here," he called and rode up to the wall. Jim followed moaning all the way. "There's note there. Just a lot of old arch things that don't go anywhere."

"They're called 'blind arches' when they just frame a bit of wall like that and don't lead through to anything. And they're Gothic," said Billy. "Some of 'em anyway. Over in that bit they're older; the rounded tops mean they're Norman."

Jim snorted. "You a tour guide or summat? I don't give a stuff what they are. It's just a boring old ruin..."

Billy stared at him and he fell silent. He'd been about to point out an area of even older stonework where the arches were smaller, but he said nothing. Jim wouldn't have been interested in the fact that he thought they were Saxon. Old Mr Jenkins had pointed out the differences on the school trip last summer, but Jim hadn't listened. He was a dickhead like all the rest; interested in booze, fags and sex and nothing else.

Billy got off his bike and let it fall, and then walked over to the last arch. In front of it a square of stone edges gleamed out of the weeds and rank grasses, about as big as the trapdoor into his loft at home. He stamped on some of them listening for them to ring hollow. Nothing. Jim looked bored and leaned against one of the arches watching as his friend scanned the ground. Billy stamped again, then suddenly squatted down and ran his hands around the edge of something. It was a sunken square of some sort and there was a flagstone fitted into it. He took out his knife and started to scrape away the muck of centuries.

"What you doin'?" Jim whined. "There's nothin' there. Just some old stones."

Billy said nothing. Soon he'd scraped it clear, then began to look around. "Now what?!" Jim asked.

"Need a lever." He walked over to a mound of rubbish heaped in the middle of the priory's floor. A steel bar lay half buried among cans and condoms and an old fridge. "This'll do." He took it, found a lump of half charred wood and walked back to the flagstone.

Billy jammed the end of the bar into the crack his knife had opened up, kicked the wood up against it and levered down hard. The bar slipped and he fell to his knees. Jim sniggered and lit a fag. Billy ignored him and tried again. The bar began to bend, but he kept up a steady pressure and the stone shifted. Only a little at first, but he quickly shoved the bar in deeper and levered again. The flagstone lifted a little more.

"There'll be nothin' but worms and bugs and a patch of dirt," said Jim between drags.

Billy worked hard, raising the stone up and then kicking the fulcrum further in so that he could lift it higher each time he levered. Then at last, just as he was beginning to sweat and pant, he made a grab for the stone's edge and strained to lift it. His back creaked and groaned with the effort but then at last it gave way and fell backwards with a thump. Both boys stood back and stared. A black hole had opened like a toothless mouth.

"Shit!" said Jim. "What the hell's that?"

"The entrance to the undercroft," said Billy. "Coming?"

"What's down there?"

Billy Shrugged. "Coffins, perhaps. Maybe note," he grinned. "Perhaps treasure."

"No shit?"

Billy grinned again. "The monks could've kept the silver down there, or maybe the priory's funds. It'd be secure."

"Come on then. Finders keepers and I'm going first!"

Billy grabbed him. "Watch out. The steps might've gone."

They peered into the dark mouth. "Na. They're sound. Look," said Jim and set his foot on the first tread.

A cold breath suddenly wrapped him in the scents of fungus, stale earth and a sickly sweetness. "Smells like death to me." Said Billy.

Jim stepped back. "You go first then. You found it."

His friend nodded, pleased to be the first to walk where no foot had trod since the church had fallen. He stepped into darkness feeling its shadow rise up his legs as he walked down the steps, like a swimmer pacing into cold water.

At the bottom of thirteen treads he stopped, allowing his eyes to adjust to the grainy dark.

"See anything?" Jim's calling voice.

"Yeah. Nothing." He lied as, slowly, shapes bloomed from the black, taking on form. *Sarcophagi*, he thought. "Coffins," he called back up the stairs. "Stone coffins."

"No shit!"

"Come down."

Billy stepped out across a flagstoned floor while a forest of reaching stone formed a vault of branching arches high above his head. He reached the first sarcophagus. An effigy of a man slept in stone, untouched by time or hammer. *The monks must have kept them hid,* he thought. No King's man had been in here when the priory had been dissolved. No greedy, grubby, searching hands had defiled the statues of their jewels and gold. Not that he could see any gold or precious gems. *So why'd they hide it? Not just for coffins and corpses, that's for sure.*

"Billy, wait!" Jim shouted in the dark. "Where are you?"

"Over here, with the dead," he called.

"Not funny, mate," Jim said as he grabbed his arm like a drowning man and hauled himself from the lonely gloom. "What're these?"

"Like I said; coffins."

"How many are there?"

They peered into the dark and could count ten dark shapes lining the walls, like boats moored on the shores of the Styx. "Must've been a family vault. Or maybe the Priors were buried here."

"The who?"

"The head monk," Billy explained.

"Oh." He said flatly. "So, where's the treasure then?"

"Ain't this enough? No one's been here for centuries. The last one who looked on this has been dust himself for years. Just think of that! We've opened a hidden vault of secrets. Ain't that treasure enough?"

"Get lost," Jim answered thinking his friend was having a laugh. "Where's the gold?"

Billy gave up and shrugged. "Who knows? Let's keep looking."

Beyond the coffins lay a universe of dark, a perfect backdrop for the shapes and colours that bloomed in their light-starved eyes. Soon Jim was seeing phantoms and grabbed Billy's arm.

"What was that, over there? Something walked across."

"A ghost I suppose."

"Shut up, arse!"

"Well, what else could it be? There's only you and me and the dead down here."

"Look, belt up, right! I'm going back up top if you don't pack it in."

"Scared?" Billy asked with a grin.

"No! Just...you know, being careful like."

"Yeah."

They walked on, the roof bounding ahead in graceful arcs supported by columns that emerged from the dark like trees in a midnight forest. They came to a stone table set with tall candlesticks and the remains of a cloth ruined and ragged with damp and years.

"Look, treasure," said Billy.

"Do you think? What're they made of?"

"Pewter."

"What's that then?"

"Metal. A mix of lead and tin."

"Crap then."

"Na. These are sixteenth century at least. Possibly older. They must be worth a fortune."

"Yeah? Well let's have 'em then!" Jim reached to take the candlesticks but stopped when something moved in the gloom. "What was that?"

"The owner, perhaps."

Jim stepped back from the table. "Come on, let's go. We can come back tomorrow when it's light. We can bring torches too."

"You leave if you want. I'm going on."

Jim looked back across the sea of dark to where a faint grey light spilled down the stairway and his mind projected shapes and movements on the black. "Come on. It might be dangerous. You know, weak roof and that. There could be a collapse. We might get killed."

"We might," Billy agreed. "Let's go and find out."

"You're bleeding mad, you are!"

"Yeah. Coming?"

Jim had no choice. Sticking close to his mate they stepped out, sinking further and further into the dark. Soon the silence became thick and textured, buzzing and hissing in their ears like words waiting to be spoken. Both boys felt as though something quiet was following, and every now and then they thought they heard a whisper, like silk drawn slowly over glass.

"We're lost, ain't we?" he suddenly said. "We couldn't get out even if we wanted to."

Billy shrugged. "We're not lost; we just don't know where we are."

"You're bleeding hilarious, you are."

"Yeah."

They walked on, their footsteps echoing over unseen distances, and sometimes a sound like a soft tread, as though something was following would whisper into the air. Then at last a far off glimmer of light filled their eyes.

"What's that?" Jim asked, grabbing Billy's arm. "A torch?"

"Na. It's too…white. Perhaps it's the moon."

They walked forward and slowly a staircase began to rise from the darkness. "We're back where we started!" said Jim with a gasp of relief. "We've walked round in bloody circles!"

"Have we?"

"Come on! I'm getting out of here," said Jim and scrambled up the stairs. Within seconds he fell back down. "Shit!" he whispered, his eyes globing like mushrooms. "Shit!"

Billy stepped over him and cautiously climbed the stairs himself, ready to leap back into the darkness. Slowly he raised his head over the lip of the trapdoor holding his breath, not knowing what he'd see, and looked out into the high-ceilinged body of a church! It was in darkness but for moonlight pouring through high Gothic windows like ladled milk, and a tiny red light, like an eye, that hung over the dark bulk of the altar.

"Shit!" he whispered. "The priory's risen again!!"

The windows were filled with a mixture of plain and stained glass. One showed the raising of Lazarus, making Billy smile despite his fear. He stepped out into the church, noting the patterned tiles beneath his feet, and ignored the hissing and whimpering that came from Jim in the undercroft.

A high wind screeched in the branches of the surrounding wood, and draughts eddied and swirled over the floors. Perhaps it was this that masked the approach of the footsteps, but Billy turned to face a figure not three paces away.

"Nuns, not monks!!" he whispered his eyes wide, his breath gasping like a broken compressor. "I always thought it'd be monks, but it was a community of nuns."

The figure bowed her head in silence. The face was hidden in shadow but the eyes glittered like old silver. She held out her hand and Billy observed the skin, stretched dead and dry, like cracked parchment over a framework of bones. She turned and walked away, knowing he'd follow. The movement of her long, black robes stirred the air, and Billy caught a scent of dust and decay. *She smells of moonlight and shadows,* he thought, and then followed.

Jim watched him disappear into the shadows of distance, and whimpered. What should he do? Should he run back across the cellar and hope he'd eventually find the priory in ruins again? He hung suspended between fear and indecision. Time stretched itself over an agony of minutes.

Then suddenly, the night exploded into an eruption of running feet. Jim held his breath and watched as Billy burst out of the shadows and raced across the floor. He reached the trapdoor, pushed Jim ahead of him and fell into the undercroft.

"Come on!" he screamed, and grabbing Jim's arm he ran into the black. The mouth of the night had swallowed them and neither knew where they were. Behind them they could hear whispers and what sounded like quiet laughter, but they could only run on.

Jim's head was filled to the brim with terror. His breath came in tortured rasps. *"Bastard fags!"* he thought and stumbled on. Once something grabbed his hand and hung on. He could feel cold, hard fingers curling around his. There was nothing soft about them; they felt like stone, or bone. He wrenched his hand free, hanging onto Billy who ran in total silence.

Then at last, a grey light glimmered in the distance. They powered towards it, reaching for safety and the normal, boring world. It was the stairway. But where would it lead?

They reached the bottom tread, and Billy pushed Jim ahead of him. He fell up and out and into moonlight and a roofless ruin. He laughed and wept in relief. Then he turned and reached for his mate's hand.

"Come on. It's OK. We're back."

Billy smiled from the depths of the dark. A strange, sad smile. "No. You go. I can't."

"What?! Don't be an arsehole. Come on, we're almost safe!"

Billy shook his head. *"You're* safe. I'm already lost," he said and stepped back into the shadows.

Jim scrambled forward, reaching. And then he watched as other hands seized his friend and led him back into blackness.

"Billy!" he called into the dark. "Billy!" his voice echoing on nothing but cold stone and lost souls.

DR HANNAH STEVENS

Is a writer from Leicester. She holds a PhD in Creative Writing from the University of Leicester and has widely published fiction. This story was written in Yangon, Myanmar where Hannah was a writer in residence for seven months. Hannah is now in Greece continuing her writing and research projects.

BENEATH THE BLACKBERRY BUSH

She opens her eyes. Sun streams through the thin curtains and the room is bright and hot. The heat has been relentless this summer. It's September now but still stifling. Selena gets out of bed, stretches and opens the curtains. It's early for a Sunday – before eight – but the back gardens below her window are already busy.

Selena watches her next-door neighbours as they hang washing, open parasols and water scorched flowerbeds before the full heat of the day kicks in. The view used to be an oasis of green but this summer the relentless sunshine has dried the gardens to paler shades of yellow and brown.

Downstairs, Selena fills the kettle and switches it on to boil. She picks up two slices of brown bread from the bread bin and drops them into the toaster. The butter is already soft, almost liquid in the butter dish. She slides her knife through, and it meets no resistance.

Mornings are quiet since Louise left. On Sundays they used to clatter around together, hang out in their pajamas, talk, laugh and loll around. It was a shock when Selena came home that day to find Louise packed, heaving the heavy suitcase into the car: leaving her for another woman she'd met at the gym.

Selena walks through to the living room. The wooden floor feels cool beneath her feet. She peers out of the front window, to the car-less driveway and beyond to the tidy terraces on the other side of Evesham Road.

She can hardly believe the scene she made now: the shouts of disbelief, how she hammered her fists on the car as it accelerated from the drive and away towards the noise of Narborough Road.

In spite of the heat Selena folds her arms, holds herself tight. Outside the birds sing but indoors the house is silent and still. She thinks of the day ahead, the hours to fill and her friends all busy with partners, families, things to do. Selena opens the window, feels the heat in the air. Perspiration gathers on her top lip and she wipes it away with the back of her hand. The heat is oppressive and thick. Outside the air shimmers above the concrete and brick: the paving slabs must be burning already.

A couple walks past. One of them pushes a buggy, the other holds the hand of a toddler. Selena swallows. They walk slowly, keeping pace with the unsteady steps of the little person with them. They're heading towards Aylestone Meadows. She notices a bag slung over the pushchair, bulging and fat. Selena imagines that there is a picnic inside: sandwiches wrapped in silver foil, carrot sticks and cartons of juice tightly packed around frozen blue ice blocks.

The meadows would be lovely today, she thinks, at least in the shady parts. She imagines the wide-open space, the blue-sky sprawling and wide. And then she thinks of the trees, clustered, thick, the cool shade beneath them. She imagines the noise of the birds singing and the rustling of leaves as they forage in the bramble bushes for blackberries.

Selena heads back to the kitchen and pulls out two plastic tubs from the cupboard. September is good for blackberries she thinks. And today she will go and pick some.

It's 11am when Selena steps out of her front door and onto the pavement. It's a short walk to the meadows from here: it takes less than five minutes. There are already cars parked at the entrance along the scorched grass verge. Lots of people have had the same idea she thinks. Selena pushes through the blue wrought iron gates and notices the long-dried mud of the path and how it feels hard beneath her feet. Soon the path opens out on each side to fields. The grass is parched and dry and crunches as she walks. Except for the pylons, the horizon is all trees now.

There are brambles everywhere: Selena can already see them. They line the edges of the haphazard, uncoordinated fields that make up the meadows. This area is too well used, she thinks. The better blackberries will be further in, more deeply hidden in the less trodden, lesser well-known parts.

Ahead there is an outcrop of trees. The meadows were used for growing fruit during the Second World War: some of the fruit trees are still here. There are apple, pear and plum trees. Selena reaches out and runs her hands across the rough bark of one to her right. There is an apple above her, and she reaches up, plucks it from the branch. It's reddish, speckled and quite small. It feels dusty in her hand and Selena wonders if it's small because of the drought. She polishes it on her shorts as if it is a cricket ball and then she takes a bite. The apple is sweet and juicy despite its size and she finishes it in a few mouthfuls.

Selena turns, tosses the core to the ground and notices a woman approaching the trees.

'Ay up,' says the woman. Selena laughs.

'Ay up,' she says.

'Lovely day again isn't it?'

'It's really beautiful,' says Selena.

'I'm here to collect some apple wood,' the woman says. She pauses, wipes the sweat from her forehead with her palm. 'I have a rabbit and she loves to chew apple wood.' The woman positions herself beneath the apple tree, reaches up and begins to pull at the finer, lower hanging branches. They snap easily and, in a few minutes, she has a neat bundle under her arm. She stops, looks at Selena. 'Okay, well that's enough I think,' she says. 'So, are you out walking today?' She leans against the tree and gestures into the distance. 'Maybe across to the Black Horse for a pint?'

'Ahh, no, not today,' says Selena, 'I'm blackberry picking.'

'That sounds just as lovely,' says the woman, 'enjoy.' And then she turns, and Selena watches her walk across the field and disappear over the horizon. Selena has been walking for fifteen minutes now. She's crossed the field where the horses are, passed by the bridge over the river and walked along the duckboards flanked on each side by tall, lush plants. It's a floodplain here - pretty much a swamp – and so in spite of the heat and the lack of rain, the plants still flourish.

Selena continues to follow the wooden path and its curves to the left and then right. She's in the middle of the city but you'd never know it here. The air is still and quiet. She hasn't seen anyone else for a while. Ahead Selena can see the flanking plants begin to clear. Beneath her feet the wooden path fades to loose stones and then to baked mud and grass. Further on the river is ahead lapping a low bank like a miniature beach. Selena stops. This has always been her favourite place. Louise and her would often bring a picnic, a bottle of wine and sit for hours talking, paddling, watching electric-blue dragonflies. For a second the scene blurs. Selena wipes her eyes and then continues to walk. Here: this is the spot, she thinks. Selena stops, takes off her backpack and pulls out the tubs she'd packed earlier. The tracks aren't so worn here, less mud and more grass. It's a smaller enclosed field surrounded by tall trees and bramble bushes thick like hedges. Despite the dry summer the brambles have thrived.

Wide green leaves cover thick, spiky chords of bramble stems. The leaves are dusty through lack of rain but still the green is dark and rich. Selena carefully pulls back the leaves to reveal the blackberries beneath. They are clustered together, interspersed with smaller leaves and sharp, thick thorns. The berries are fat and ripe: dark purple, almost black. The sun suits them, she thinks.

Carefully Selena begins to pull the berries from the tangled stems. They are soft, so ripe and full of liquid. She puts one into her mouth. A little pressure from her tongue and the berry bursts. It is sweet. Selena swallows and licks her lips.

It doesn't take her long to fill the tubs from her bag. Her hands are purple now, covered in the sticky juice of those too ripe to pull free in one clean piece. She already has too many for one person but the more she picks, the more she finds, and it is difficult to stop, to think of them falling, going to waste. Maybe she will make a crumble, a pie too. And maybe add some to vodka like Louise used to like. She thinks of drinking it alone this winter and then pushes the thought from her mind.

Selena continues to fill the tub in her hand. She doesn't stop when the berries reach the brim. Maybe she'll just carry this one home in her arms, rather than replace the lid and limit the ones she can collect.

She's standing beneath a tall oak tree. The shade is nice, and she doesn't want to stop yet. The pile is becoming precarious now, but she picks a few more. The pyramid topples and some of the blackberries fall. Selena watches as they roll across her feet and onto the floor below. The undergrowth is dark but something light, a pale kind of pink catches her eye.

Selena kneels down, pushes the brambles away. It takes her a few minutes to realise what she's looking at. It's a baby squirrel – tiny and hairless but perfectly formed. For a few seconds she doesn't move. It must've fallen from a nest in the tree above. Selena looks around but cannot see a worried mother squirrel searching for her baby. Is it even still alive? It was difficult to tell from this distance, especially with something so small.

Selena leans forward, reaches out and brushes the squirrel's head with her little finger. It feels warm, though cooler than it perhaps should.

'I probably shouldn't touch you,' she says out loud, 'in case your mum is looking for you. Except that I don't think she is.' Gently, Selena picks up the squirrel. It is so light and fits easily into the palm of her hand. Its skin is smooth and soft against hers. She cups it in her hand and moves it closer towards her. Now it is near she can see the movement of its chest, delicate and slight. Selena sits down on the grass. Maybe she should wrap it in a handkerchief or similar?

Something to keep it warm. Except she doesn't have one and does it feel cooler now than it did a moment ago? Yes, it does she thinks. And now she knows that there is nothing she can do.

Selena sits cross-legged, the baby squirrel cupped in her palm, held close to her chest. She has never watched anything die before. Not like this. And then she begins to cry. The tears feel hot on her face and her chest heaves.

Selena sits there for a long time and watches the shadows grow as the sun falls. The little body in her palm is much cooler now. She should probably leave soon. Selena places the baby squirrel back beneath the blackberry bush. The delicate peach of the body looks so vulnerable against the backdrop of earth: exposed. She knows that it is probably silly, but she cannot bear to leave it this way.

Selena gathers a small handful of soil. It's difficult in this weather when the earth is so dry and hard, and it takes her a few minutes. There are some dead leaves too: camouflage brown. Finally, she covers the small body with the debris she has gathered. There is just enough coverage to obscure the pinkness: to hide it mostly from view.

Selena stands, rubs the soil from her hands. At home she will wash the blackberries and pile them into glass bowls along the work surface in her kitchen. Afterwards she will take a handful, put them into her mouth and then savour the sweetness on her tongue.

CATHY MANSELL

Author of romantic suspense. Five books published with Tirgearr Publishing. Cathy's early work, short stories, articles featured in national magazines. She prepared the Anthology, "Taking Off" supported by Arts Council UK, by Lutterworth Writers', of which she is President. A two book deal with Headline, the first, A Place To Belong arrives November 2019.

LEICESTER MARKET

Over 800 years old, Leicester Market is still the pivotal point in the city with easy access to the town's many shopping areas. It is the largest outdoor covered market in Europe with over 270 stalls and a separate meat, fish and poultry market.

When I first came across this amazing market, it was the mid-1960s. I'd travelled first from Ireland and then Birmingham to settle in Leicester. My late husband was in the hosiery trade and Leicester was the place to be.

The market in the centre of Leicester struck me, back then, as a colourful, vibrant place where people went for cheap fruit and vegetables. I'd seen nothing quite like it before. You could walk through the large open market, drool over the freshness of the fruit and drink in the smells of an array of colourful fruits and vegetables arranged in rows displaying the produce to its advantage. It must have taken ages to set up, but to experienced hands, like these traders, it was an art and their livelihood. Gary Lineker's family had a stall here at one time, and he worked on the stall as a teenager.

Alongside fruit and vegetables, the market had a range of stalls from clothing to household stuff where you could buy almost anything from coats to boots for the working man, to the latest fashion for the ladies and children. You could pick up a lipstick on the cosmetic stall, toys for children and a variety of everyday goods.

I've known people to shop on the market for variety and price and carry their produce home on the bus rather than shop in a supermarket.

Many a time I've travelled into Leicester just to get my meat fresh from the meat market. So different to buying from the local butcher. The display of different makes of sausage, cold meats and raw meat is amazing. The traders have time for a joke and a laugh and are helpful when you want advice on the best cut for roasting. It's a place of great character and atmosphere and a walk through Leicester market will guarantee a smile at the banter of the stall holders as they hold the customers attention with their bartering. At one time hot food was available such as mushy peas and sausage and a cup of tea. Now there are no shortage of places in and around the marketplace where food is served daily.

The 1850 Corn Exchange is a fascinating place, a focal point in the market square and I soon discovered it to be a Grade 11 listed building with an impressive stone staircase forming an archway over the top. It is where farmers and merchants once traded corn and grain. The stairway now forms the entrance to a trendy public house. It also has a statue outside to the Duke of Rutland.

In the 70s my son had to cross Leicester Market to catch a bus to English Martyrs school and could never resist stopping for a chat with the stall holders on his way home, often missing his bus, giving me cause for worry. At sixteen he was offered a Saturday job on the men's clothing stall. Surprised that he liked it so much, I would call at the stall, sometimes to his embarrassment, to keep an eye on him, bringing him something to eat and drink as a pretence. I guess what he loved was the banter and being in the open air with little restrictions and a few bob spending money in his pocket. He stuck it for a while until he moved on to his chosen trade.

Leicester Market is much the same today as it was back then, a noisy exciting place where loud cries of the traders shouting their wares still echo around the marketplace. Today, you can buy almost anything from grains, pulses and spices from India to exotic fruits from the Caribbean and all the flavours of Europe.

I don't get to visit the market quite so much these days, but I have fond memories of how it was in the 60s and I'm proud to say you can still bag a bargain. It remains an exciting place, the hub in a busy city for the peoples of Leicester.

CHARLIE JONES

Is a writer from Merseyside. His poetry has appeared in Acumen, Orbis, The Honest Ulsterman, The Caterpillar, and Sentinel Literary Quarterly, as well as several other magazines and journals.

GRANDMA DOESN'T HAVE TIME TO DIE

Don't you worry about me, me duck.
Don't you worry about Grandma.
I don't have time to die.
I've got to make up the beds
And sweep under the stairs
And peel the potatoes for tea.
There's dandelions in the garden that need pulling
And sheets that need hanging.
I've got bills to pay
And prescriptions to pick up
And magazines to take round to Auntie Joan.
There's flowers on the side for Grandpa
And my piano won't play itself.
If I died, nothing would get done.
So don't you worry about me, me duck,
I don't have time to die.

PAM THOMPSON
WATCHING – BRADGATE PARK

I watch the young buck grazing,
the way he moves, unalarmed by my presence,
and turns, walks away, lifting each elegant leg.

As he eats, he lifts his head, watches an oak,
mostly green but with a few yellow leaves,
the way the wind moves its branches.

The oak watches the monument –
shaped like a tankard, on the hill in the distance –
and people sitting on the rocks.

The monument watches the woods,
the fences around the woods – it will always be vigilant.
Remembers how soldiers set the fences on fire.

It watches me but its eyes are clouded,
– so much has crowded into those eyes:
the dying, the dead, the joyful; the battering rain.

YEVGENY SALISBURY

Born in North Wales, Yevgeny moved to Leicester ten years ago, where he dropped out of a PGCE but joined Leicester Writers' Club. He is President of the club for a second time and also runs a primary school writers' club. Yevgeny is a spoken word performer and visual artist.

LANDSCAPES OF LOSS

In the end you come to understand about death. A bit. When I got the text, I don't know why I didn't stand in my flat – stay leaning against the door – to make the call. I went out into the yard round the side, where, behind the high brick walls, the lads and even grown men go to smoke without their families seeing. I met a guy there once rolling up who swore he was about to go on the Hajj and that would be the end of the tobacco and the weed. To be fair, I haven't seen him since. He said his friends called him crazy.

My yard was empty. An overcast November day. I'm sobbing on the phone. When the funeral's arranged, I'll get another text with the details. Then silence. And all around is only Highfields and a grey sky.

Highfields is named for its past landscape. Today it has a park you can sledge down and smaller children look bonny in the longer grass in high summer and there is a concrete slab where some kind of bandstand used to be and a lump of marble that used to be a fountain and very early one morning I picked up broken glass from round this fountain while waiting for the transit of something – perhaps Venus – except the clouds were too persistent and all I saw were vitreous offerings to the god of lonely wanderings, stolen again and again by my cold fingers and thrown into the bin, and this jogger comes round and pauses to watch me like I'm crazy as a pothead in someone else's yard. But I suppose I'm just interested in planets.

I stood between the high brick houses on my own street one night looking up at Jupiter, and a young English woman, who honest to god looked like a hooker and a drug addict, stopped and asked me what me I was looking at and then we looked at it together. She said she'd had no idea you could see other planets. She asked how I knew it was Jupiter and I said because it was so bright, and it was the right time and the right part of the sky and then I admitted the main way I can tell Jupiter is by its stripes. I can't see the stripes themselves even with binoculars, but they do something stripy to the reflected light and I asked my dad when I was a kid what the stripy star was, and he was astonished.

There are moments beneath stars and planets that are cut out of time. Beneath clouds the only moment is the present moment and this is what I suddenly understand about death as I pocket my phone in my yard and am aware in that moment it is a Victorian yard and I know the late nineteenth century either never existed or exists only in the present, like everything else. Like the dead body of my best friend. Like the train about to pull into the station in town that was meant to take me to visit him. Like our plans for the weekend.

Well, the days pass. It's a Catholic funeral and I think it's almost worth becoming a Catholic to get a funeral like that with the choir and the communion cups. And then I'm back in Leicester, wandering up and down New Walk, asking myself is this the essence of my city? Are we different, are we special, because we have devoted one whole spoke of our civic wheel to the pedestrian? No bicycles.

The weekend after the funeral, I buy a coffee table on ebay and must collect it from Cambridge. I take the train. In Cambridge, a brass band drifts by on a punt. I get chatting to a beggar who tells me she too is from Leicester, from the Belgrave Road. She looks more council house than Golden Mile, but then again there are surely some council houses round there too because I knew someone once who got moved there from Beaumont Leys.

'Is there still the clock tower in the centre?' the beggar lady asks me.

'They haven't knocked it down?'

'Of course not!' I say and she laughs like it was a foolish concern; like no one would even think of making TK Max the centre of their city. Though the clock tower is in a bit of an odd place. Like, when my friend was still alive, I tried to show off my city to him and he concluded that there was nothing there. I had shown him the cathedral, the Guildhall, New Walk, the magazine, the town hall and the clock tower and I was insulted and deflated. I garbled something pat about the people making the city and it all being about the festivals and the live-and-let-live attitude and the easy, unprejudiced use of ethnic labels and how since moving here I no longer feel I must insist I'm Welsh when I'm mislabeled English because in Leicester being English, whilst mildly associated with being a crack-head – at least in Highfields – does not imply bigotry and imperialism.

My friend was an ardent left-liberal and so suitably impressed and yet I'm caught between his words somehow, like Leicester must have denied itself a centre and spread itself thinly by placing its clock tower so ambitiously far from other points of interest. The triangulated centre it creates is the fish market, bright and new but lacking in both architectural merit and local relevance – the sea is not nearby – or it is Molly O'Grady's, but Molly's, a cheerful and accepting "fighting pub" – a fight almost every Saturday – has been replaced now by a swanky bar with a picture-window, with a view of the back of that same fish market. So, the centre of the city, perhaps, is the new statue of a Suffragette, also round the back of the fish market. My friend never saw our new statue of a Suffragette. My friend never answers me now out loud and the only opinions he expresses are the ones he has shown me a thousand times; good words, but always the same. Though is that not enough for anyone?

In Venice last summer, I met a Parisienne Intellectual who said she wanted to visit Leicester and I told her there was nothing there and she said she really, really wanted to visit Leicester. It's like that advert the city took out in Uganda in '72 to dissuade the Ugandan Asians from moving to Leicester in the hour of their need. It turns out if you tell people your streets aren't paved with gold, they come to create a Golden Mile for you. I have high hopes of my Parisienne Intellectual. She's into modern art and we could do with a dedicated modern art gallery. This is a flippant comment, but you can say what the hell you like when you're running mad with grief. I think I might be. After on Sunday going to Cambridge for a coffee table, on Wednesday I went to Brixworth for a coffee table and I now have two coffee tables and the lighter one balances on my bed all day and on my computer all night and the heavier one stands on end with its legs around a stack of books. It's a very small flat. I'm hoping to move and then I can invite people in and give them coffee and they will see from my coffee tables I am a man of discernment. I'll use one as a TV stand, or they'll see from my proliferation of coffee tables that I'm a nutter.

When Raskolnikov was sent half mad by the near endless St Petersburg summer days, he ended up a murderer. This is pointless. You can't change history by prefiguring it. People die.

I walk into town for my work's Christmas do at a restaurant. It's dark and it's drizzling. The quickest way is down New Walk. I close my eyes for fifty steps. I check I'm not in the gutter and then close my eyes for another thirty steps. I pass the museum with its rather pedestrian columns. I pass the Catholic church with its high brick walls. In town there are the lights. An ordinary tree weeps falling stars. The restaurant is just round the corner from Molly's and I tell a colleague how I used to live and work there when it was still Molly's and how the biggest trouble was always when the lights went up at four in the morning and women would spot their boyfriends dancing with other women and

I could never get why the rivals would end up half killing each other over some ugly, cheating, no-account bloke.

In the restaurant, I sit next to a colleague whose son died a few months back. She asks me about the house I want to buy in Beaumont Leys. It's a one-up-one-down just over the brow of the hill, so if you stood on the roof you could probably see Old John at the top of Bradgate Park gifted-to-the-people-of-Leicestershire-in-perpetuity-for-their-quiet-enjoyment-or-words-to-that-effect, from where you can see the start of the flatlands that stretch all the way to Russia. Why the fuck would I want to see that? Like an endless summer day. I remember when my colleague showed me photos on her phone of where she scattered her son's ashes by the shores of the North Sea, the unrequited love of the people of Leicester, who I think must once have lived out there when it was still land or why do we yearn for so cold an embrace? I say "we", but in all honesty, my sea is still the Irish Sea, so I probably fail to be yet, quite, truly Leicester. I yearn for Snowdonia, for Anglesey, for yr Hen Wlad ar lan y mor.

But then, half of Leicester has merely washed up here from somewhere else, just like Saint Dwynwen, Welsh patron saint of love, who stumbled lovelorn ashore on Llanddwyn Island.

My friend was thirty-one and about to get married. My colleague's son was in his twenties and about to become a father. You would think my colleague and I would have more important things to talk about than the housing market; more definite places to send our wishes than out to sea. My mind should rest on a hospital bed, hers on a mangled car. Instead we rove restlessly out into the ever changing, ever mocking waves, or off into this speculative future where I have my own house back in LE4. I've lived in LE1, LE2, LE3 and LE4, or think I have living in the present makes it hard to tell; escaping into the future makes it hard to care.

At the end of the evening, another colleague offers me a lift home and I accept. She then admits she's forgotten where she parked her car. We walk around. It's a weeknight so not much is open. We pass the end of Market Street, which is where the Oxfam shop is where I once met a man who invited me to a Spanish class that was meant to be for the over sixties. I went every week and was told that if anyone official came in I had to pretend to be the tutor. The man who had invited me was an enthusiastic polyglot and the star of the class, but then he became repetitive and incoherent and then he died of a brain tumour. But this is years ago so caught in the brick-wall flatness of spent time. Market Street is also where I used to take coffee with an ex-alcoholic who looked a bit like Stephen Mackintosh – a pleasant-looking TV actor of the day who could cry like a wounded angel. The ex-alcoholic, however, was a hard case and a liar and a cheat. I never saw him cry. We took coffee because he owed me money and I was slowly getting it back by the cupful with milk and sugar, while listening to him trying to talk me into lending him more. I gave him a hat, he gave me an umbrella, so we're quits on the outdoor apparel score, but the bastard still owes me a hundred quid and things got a little tense in the end, especially as he started acting like I was the one owed him, and it is with trepidation I peer into Market Street in case, even at this late hour and in December, there he is haunting it. He is not.

We walk past the Adoption Bureau and The Youth Court, this part of town being something of a one-stop-shop for troubled starts in life, and when we loop back on ourselves, and end up on Hotel Street, outside Molly's-that-was, I start thinking about the old guy I got chatting to at the bar who said he only became a murderer because he was raped when he was eight. I wonder if he'll ever get to an age where he stops making excuses. Personally, I've never murdered anyone yet and my best friend never did his whole life through. I remember that conversation too, back at university. Kind of thing you don't forget.

And I remember the Bar Manager losing fifty quid in next door's fruit machine – not even our own fruit machine – and when the landlady's drunk son put a fist through a window and cut an artery and wandered around squirting blood everywhere until we persuaded him to accept first aid and then he wanted to sleep it off and refused to believe he'd wake up dead. It took seven policemen to get him into the ambulance. I had to clean up the blood. So, then I end up in this heart-to-heart with him and he told me about losing his dad and how it affected him when he was little. I liked the guy. We shared a house for a while on Tudor Road, but he rarely slept there because of the bed bugs. Honest to god, they got on my wick too and I lost patience in the end and fumigated the lot of them, which I suppose does make me a murderer of sorts after all. The worst thing is when you pick them off your skin with their legs all waving about and they explode between your fingers and you don't know whether to feel bad that you've spilt blood or indignant that it's your own blood. I was in love at the time, though, so didn't care about anything much except staring at maps of the city wishing I could walk up to the door of my beloved's house, but it was unrequited so all I could do was stare at the maps and at the blank wall of my attic room where I wanted to stick up loads of photos of the guy but I didn't have any and it would have looked psycho and the landlord didn't allow blue-tack. I told my best friend about my beloved on the phone but was afraid of being boring because I managed to remain aware that lovers can be dull. And I did paint a picture of my beloved but then I hid it in my wardrobe and on display instead had a painting of my ex-girlfriend because that made me look straight and I was going through a phase of being set upon and hit and stuff and I just wanted an easy life. It was a hot summer and I spent a lot of time lying on my bed staring at the skylight, killing my only company between repentant-indignant fingers. It seemed to be perpetually four in the morning and already too light. At one point I did make it out of the city: I went to Llanddwyn Island to scratch initials in the sand.

My friend and I went on a few holidays, always on a budget, so always sharing a room. He slept with his hands folded on his chest in an attitude of prayer, except for when he dreamt, he was being chased by giant wasps, when he would leap up screaming. Once he jumped out of a window onto a flat roof and woke there perplexed. He said one of the things he prayed for before he slept, apart from world peace and that, was that he would not dream of giant wasps.

One time we stayed in bunk beds in a place where you had to pay extra for bedding, and we didn't have extra to pay so we slept under nothing but our pillows and I for one lay there thinking about the Swedish military and the body's propensity to get used to cold. This was on a trip to Rome, where the nights were cold but the days hot and my friend kept stopping to drink from fountains because he was a health-freak and wanted to stay hydrated. But we did see the sights. I cried in the Pantheon because it was like being inside a universe curtailed and because it's old and that seemed to matter at the time; he prayed for many minutes in St Peter's. Funnily enough, he did get followed for several minutes by a huge hornet on that holiday, while I was on tenterhooks he'd turn around and see it. He didn't and maybe that is tantamount to a prayer answered. And yet why go anywhere, even as far as Oxfam on Market Street, if only to find your best stories affixed to a corpse?

My friend had known he was ill for weeks but not that it was serious until near the end, so he hadn't told me a thing until the night he rang to say he had only months left to live. We no longer lived anywhere near each other but agreed to meet up nine days later. He said he was still well enough to show me around a museum where he once volunteered. We chatted for forty minutes. We cried a bit. He said he was scared. I reminded him some of his favourite people died in their thirties – Ayrton Senna, Princess Diana, Jesus – and this cheered him up considerably. 'Yes!' he said. 'We can do this!'

Instead of meeting up, nine days after he called me, he was dead. You know, perhaps I'll think of that if I ever make it onto the roof of my new house and look across to Bradgate Park, where Lady Jane Gray once lived, who was the Nine Day Queen. And that really isn't crass, because she too was real enough. I think. I do start to think even my friend was once real enough and I should dare to let the past become less flat, less nothing. I should give it back perhaps a little of its geography, allow it to make its pilgrimages and fold its nervous hands.

So, my colleague has finally found her car in sight of Molly's and she drives me up to Highfields, where the bricks mark out the sky, and I loved my friend, I know I did. I'm not demonstrative like he was. I wrote a poem for him – for the dead him – about all our conversations over the years and our last exchange of text messages the day before he died. I called it "And You".

'God bless you,' you would say;
I would say, 'And you.'

'I love you,' you would say;
I would say, 'And you.'
And on what was to be, perhaps, our last meeting
I thought I'd finally dare to say all that I was feeling
That I did love you.

A smiley after "see you soon" was all the hint I gave;
"I cannot wait to see you" was your last wave.

MAHSUDA SNAITH

Is the winner of the SI Leeds Literary Prize and Bristol Short Story Prize. Her debut novel 'The Things We Thought We Knew' was published in 2017 when she was named an 'Observer New Face of Fiction'. Her second novel 'How to Find Home' was serialised on BBC Radio 4.

THE WORLD IN ONE STREET

The street wondered who the new shop owner was. Each morning, they watched her open the shutters on 38b before slipping under and rolling them down again. The halal butcher said he saw her slide a suitcase in once, big as a toddler but light enough to lift with one hand.

It was not like them to intrude, so they carried on with their businesses. Ring binders, bangles, sauerkraut, massages, coffee and kebabs. Yet they couldn't help but observe the flamboyant colours of the new shop owner's scarves and how her electric blue hair changed style every day. They noted her olive skin and dark eyes but none of them, not even the Turkish café owner who had lived in five countries, could identify her ethnicity.

Their curiosity began to gnaw at them.

"Welcome to our street," they said as she walked past.

She smiled but never replied. They decided this was because she was new to the country so spoke to her in their own languages; Punjabi, Hindi, Gujarati, Turkish, Swahili, Mandarin, German, Polish and more. Still, she gave no reply. They did not mind; she had such friendly eyes.

One day, a researcher arrived from the London School of Economics. She told the street that Narborough Road was, perhaps, the most diverse street in the UK. She had already found shop owners originating from 22 countries.

"This really is the world in one street," she told them. "Everyone working cheek to jowl in perfect harmony. It's remarkable."

It was the Canadian bookseller who told them the television crew were coming (he always found out these things first). The Sweet Mart decorated its windows as though it was Diwali. The Zambezian shop owner ordered a brighter range of fabrics. The Chinese restaurant erected a new illuminated sign. In all the hubbub, they forgot about the shop owner with the electric blue hair and the way her shutters had remained down since the researcher had arrived.

It was a few days before filming that one of them, nobody would say who, knocked on the shutters of 38b. When there was no answer, they crept down the alley of the shop and found the back door was ajar. The building was empty except for a purple suitcase left open in the middle of the shop floor. Inside were thirteen passports.

It wasn't long before the passports were being circulated up and down the street. Everyone marvelled at the thirteen identities and thirteen different countries of origins that lay within. And the thirteen photographs! Each woman with a different hair colour, some with headdresses, some with scarves wrapped elaborately around their necks, some with red lips and perfect winged eyeliner, some with arched brows and piercings, some with none, but all of them with the same dark eyes they had each found so endearing.

When the television crew came, the street did not tell them about the woman and her passports. It was really not like them to intrude.

TREVOR GLYN LOCKE

Was the founder of Arts in Leicester and now publishes Music in Leicester, both online magazines about the music life of the city. Trevor is also a novelist, poet and non-fiction writer. He was born in Portsmouth but has lived in Leicester longer than he has anywhere else.

THE SOCIAL HISTORY OF LEICESTER AS SEEN THROUGH ITS LIVE MUSIC

In this article, I look back at the popular music of Leicester between the years 2007 and 2017. That's ten years during which I was going out to see bands. By the start of that period, I had already been writing about popular music for some three to four years. So, as a music journalist, I had my feet firmly under the desk. It was also a period during which I was writing about the history of Leicester, as seen through its buildings, streets and open spaces. Few people have written anything about the history of music in our city. Later on, I will look back, even further, into the history of music in our city.

Why music? Well, from a social history point of view, music tells us a lot about a community. Looking at how people were entertained gives us insights into the life and times of an era just, as much as what people were eating, the clothes they wore, the films they watched, their politics and other aspects of life which were characteristic of the time. I will return to that theme later. For now, let me get on.

The popular music scene in this city, was a vibrant one in 2007. By then, I had started to write about music on a more or less daily basis. Most of what I wrote was published in the magazine Arts in Leicestershire. That year saw the start of what I called the 'great golden age of indie.' Not only were there numerous bands in the city but also bands were coming here to play from all over Britain - even from America. The most notable gig of 2007 was when one of the biggest USA rock bands, of the time, decided to play at The Shed. The band called Boy Hits Car came over from Los Angeles to tour the small venues of the UK. They thought that would put them back in touch with their fans, after having played huge festivals and arena-level concerts for so many years. They wanted to get back to the coal-face of real music by playing in tiny venues. That event took place on the 3rd December. By then, they were, for me, one of my favourite bands. I worshipped and adored them. I played their records constantly. So, to have them standing in front of me, just inches away, was an incredible experience. Imagine yourself standing next to the Beatles or the Rolling Stones.

As a city, Leicester has always been under-rated for its music scene. Contrary to this, there are those that have celebrated the contribution made by musicians from Leicester to the national music scene. In particular, the contribution of artists from Leicester's African and Caribbean communities have been of national importance.

It's all about the venues?

Music is often based on venues. Places where music is performed on a regular basis. Leicester has, for a long time, benefited from having a large number of long-running music venues. Some much-loved venues have been lost. The one that readily comes to the mind was The Attik. A small property situated down a little side road called Free Lane, off Halford Street. Another one was Lock42 which was part of the building occupied by Stayfree, overlooking the banks of the canal, in Frog Island. Some might also remember Sub 91 opening in Granby Street, above what was then the Walkabout bar.

Here are some of the venues that most people will remember, some of which are still running. The Shed was my 'home' venue at the time. The small property in Yeoman Street was where I spent most of my evenings. It is now the longest-serving venue in Leicester, having opened in 1994. But I also frequented most of the other venues in the city. The Musician started in the year 2000, which saw Darren Nockles take over the Bakers Arms in Wharf Street South, a public house that had been active since the 1970s, turning it into the venue we know today as The Musician. The old Musician closed its doors on 31st December 2004 only to re-opened in 2005. In its time the Charlotte was the city's main venue for touring bands and some of the most important bands played there. It began putting on live music when it was called The Princess Charlotte. The last full year of the venue was 2006. It closed in 2009. The Donkey, a pub in Welford Road, became a music venue in 2005. In the following year, Gaz Birtles began working there as a promoter. Some might remember Gaz as a member of the popular band called The Swinging Laurels. These were the city's permanent live music venues. Gigs also took place at The Criterion, in Millstone Lane, and at a new venue in Wellington Street called The Basement Bar, where I put on shows. I also put on gigs at a pub in Church gate called The Sun. There were also a few gigs at a little bar called Maddisons, not far from The Shed. Occasionally, music shows were held at the YMCA Theatre in East Street. Apart from the venues, live music was also put on for customers at a wide variety of pubs. They would offer live bands, usually on a Friday night. For a while, I helped to organise shows at the Pavilion, the cafe on Victoria Park.

From time to time, bands from Leicester would play at out-of-town gigs. Camden was a favourite destination for local bands that wanted to get gigs out of the city. Leicester bands played at Tommy Flynns, Bar Monsta, Bar Fly, Koko, Underworld and The Dublin Castle. They also performed at The Fly, in New Oxford Street. Birmingham was another destination for our bands when they went on tour. A Birmingham venue that played host to our bands on a regular basis was Scruffy Murphys. Other than long trips away, city bands also played in Hinckley, Coalville, Melton Mowbray and sometimes Loughborough.

Going back further in time, many readers will also remember the part played in the music life of Leicester by The Palais (in Humberstone Gate), The Bear Cage, The Il Rondo, Baileys, Helsinki and even further back than that The Alhambra Music Hall and the Opera House in Silver Street. Not all of these places were live music venues but there was a time when musical tastes gravitated towards the work of singers and music hall variety acts. Why some of these venues closed, we might never know. But we must not forget the many shows and concerts held at the De Montfort Hall and the Granby Halls (demolished in 2001.) The Who played there on the opening night of their tour on 25th January 1981. Many gigs at these places are still the stuff of legend in the minds of Leicester people.

People who went to gigs

When I look at the photos that were taken in the period 2007 to around 2009, I see a lot of young faces. Audiences during the noughties were composed mainly of teenagers and people in their early twenties. It varied according to the style of music. Older fans tended to like punk, some metal and the line-ups of bands that played cover songs (the hit tunes of well-known groups and singers.) Weekend gigs, at the pubs, tended to offer bands that played songs from the time when the older customers were young. The youngsters were more interested in contemporary styles of music, in particular, the bands that played their own music, rather than covers of classic tunes from the great bands of the past. Most of the young bands, from that time, were unsigned and they usually wrote their own music, which they played at the gigs.

Which bands?

The thing that stands out about Leicester, during this so-called 'golden era', was that it had many bands. Many, many bands. In fact, I once wrote that

'Leicester has more bands, per head of population than most other cities of comparable size.' I collected bands like other people collect stamps. I kept lists of bands. In those days, there were hundreds of them.

The majority of the groups I went to see comprised teenage musicians. I sometimes joked that there must be something in Leicester's water supply that engendered musicality in the youthful population. More seriously, I suspected that our schools were a lot better at teaching music in those days. A lot of the young musicians came from the same schools. Names like Beauchamp, Bosworth, Countesthorpe, Guthlaxton, Wigston, even Leicester Grammar School, cropped up continually. There was a time when you could walk through the city centre and every other kid you saw had a guitar case slung over his back. Many of the musicians were at the colleges and, when they played at gigs, they brought their fans with them. In large numbers. Look at the audiences, at any gig in the city, back then, and you would mostly see kids aged 17 to 20. Not true of today's shows. Most audiences, these days, are older.

The bands I most remember from this period include Set in Stone, Aikon, The Chairmen, M48, The Codes, The Displacements, The Heroes, Freefall Felix, The Lowreys and Autohype. All of these have disappeared now. A few of the musicians that were in them are still around, performing with new groups. But many have disappeared from the local scene. Take Set in Stone, for example. The lead singer of that band was Steve Faulkner. He is still performing, as a soloist, at venues or private parties. Very few of the bands that played during the period are still around. The most notable exceptions are Skam, The Fazed and Ferris. These are bands that have a track record of twenty years or more. Many of the younger bands were short-lived. As their members turned eighteen, most of them left Leicester to take up places at other universities. Few returned to our city to continue their musical activities. There are always some for whom music is in their blood. These are the ones who cannot give up the thrill of the public performance.

They were all local lads playing home-grown music. To my ears, most of their music was every bit as good as what you heard on Top of the Pops, or on the radio's rundown of the top 40. I knew all of the band members personally and wrote about them all. But, like hundreds of other people, I loved their music. Most of these bands had a knack of writing catchy tunes and memorable melodies. I would often go home, from a gig, humming the tunes I had heard that night or whistling them as I walked.

When it came to indie bands, it was youth that predominated. Musicians as young as fifteen could be seen on the city's stages. Because Leicester had so many bands, there were numerous rehearsal rooms and recording studios. An industry grew up to serve the interests of the thriving music scene. Shops that sold guitar strings did a roaring trade. Printers were kept busy catering for the demand for flyers, posters and album sleeves. Some of the recording studios that served the bands back then are still in use today. For the fans of popular music, there were quite a few music shops selling records. Ainsley is one that many people will remember. Some of them sold CDs produced by the local bands. The musician and writer John Barrow remembers a music shop called Humbuckers where he purchased his first saxophone, in 1974.

Most of these local bands recorded music they had composed. I have a collection of several hundred CDs made by Leicester bands. These I have painstakingly classified and catalogued and hope to donate the collection to a library that can curate them. Much of that valuable archive would have been lost. People keep records for many years, but they are in private collections, not accessible to researchers and the public. Some recordings have been lost forever; they were uploaded to the Internet, to platforms that have gone. Local music is often ephemeral but, in my view, it has interest for historians or music enthusiasts and should be preserved.

Music of the fields

Not all music was played inside buildings. During the decade, covered by this article, festivals were also an important part of the city's and county's music offerings. As they still are today. The Summer Sundae festival attracted music fans from all over the country. Established in 2001, the festival was held in the grounds of the De Montfort Hall and was a key part of the city's annual music programme. It offered stage-time not only to the big national names but also to the new, up-and-coming groups. It grew from being a one-day event to being a weekender running from Friday to Sunday. The last event was held in 2012. In its place, a new festival was established. Simon Says began in 2013. In the same year, the Hand Made festival began, based at Leicester University and then the O2 Academy building. The O2 arena had its first show in 2010, the headline Act being the singer and hip-hop artist Professor Green.

Originally, the Hand Made event took place in the city centre venues. In 2013, it was held at The Firebug, The Peoples' Photographic Gallery, Duffy's Bar, The Cookie Jar and The Guildhall. In May 2015, the festival moved to the University of Leicester campus.

Abbey Park also played host to a cycle of outdoor events and the Abbey Park Festival became an important staging post for many of the city's bands. Founded in 1981, the festival, held in Abbey Park, went on for another twenty years as a key part of the city's annual music programme. In 2009, Leicester band Autohype played to a crowd of over 20,000 at Abbey Park's bonfire night. A similar-sized crowd was present in 2014 when rising pop stars, The Vamps were the headline act, supported by local artists Jonezy and Curtis Clacey. Many music fans will have happy memories of those events. For many local bands, playing at this festival gave them the recognition that otherwise might have taken years to achieve.

In 2005, a new festival was founded, in the Leicestershire village of Wymeswold. Glastonbudget began as a programme of tribute bands and rapidly grew to also include what it called 'original bands', those playing their own music. It is still going today. The Glastonbudget festival has grown into one of the county's premier music events and attracts thousands of people from all over the country.

Strawberry Fields festival, held at a fruit farm near Coalville, also attracted national acts as well as the small, unsigned groups from the local area and further afield. Download became established as the big national event for the metal crowd, although it was just over the border of Leicestershire in Castle Donnington. There were many smaller festivals held within the city boundaries. We saw the rise of Oxjam - a national series of festivals held to raise money for the Oxfam charity. Leicester's Oxjam became one of the biggest in the country and is still going today.

Music has always been an important part of the Leicester Caribbean carnival. After the parade, a stage on Victoria Park provided a range of music acts during the afternoon. Many of the floats that wound their way through the streets of the city centre had mobile sound systems, providing music for the dancers that followed them. Another park-based festival that has been part of the city's annual celebrations is Gay Pride. Also held on Victoria Park, Pride has always featured musical acts on its main stage. Recently, the headline act was the Leicester singer Sam Bailey. More recently, the City Festival has seen a live music stage set up in Jubilee Square. Annual music festivals were held in many parts of Leicestershire. These county events provided opportunities for bands and singers to get their work out to entirely new audiences.

So far, we have looked at the music of modern times. But music has always been an important part of the life of this city as far back as we wish to go. I have published a series of articles about music from the time of Richard III, the music of the Tudors, the rise of the music halls in Victorian times and music between the world wars. It is not easy to say what Leicester people listened to in medieval times, but we can get some idea from the surviving evidence. We can go back even further than that.

What did the Romans ever play for us?

As part of my writing about Leicester music, through history, I came up with an article about music when the Romans ran the city. That was probably from the first century up to the end of the fourth century. There are no surviving records of what music the Romans played for us in Leicester. But we do know about the music of the Romans generally. From that, we can work out what kind of tunes the people of the town listened to, the kind of instruments they were played on, when and where such music was heard. When the Romans were in charge, our town was not called Leicester. They called the place Ratae Corieltauvorum. In the Domesday Book, it was recorded as Ledecestre, based on the name given to it by the Saxons.

Over the past few years, I have been plotting the course of music in Leicester from Roman times onwards. One particularly interesting question I got into was 'when King Richard III was here, what music did he listen to?' We know a lot more about the music in the times of the last of the Plantagenets than we do about that of the Romans. We know that Richard spent a few days at Leicester Castle in 1483. It is likely that musicians played for him, during that stay, when he hosted a large banquet. Apart from doing high-society shows, travelling players also visited the city, during medieval times, to entertain folk in the streets. Some were known as Troubadours. Others were called The Waits. The Waits originally went from one place to another to play for the residents but later they settled down in one locality and became the town band.

We can go through the history of Leicester sketching out what music people would have heard at any period. We know what kind of instruments were played, where and when music was performed. Right up to the time of the first recorded music. Gradually record players and radios became affordable by the majority of people. That subject is an interesting one because music tells a lot about social life at any period. From the Romans to the Tudors, from the Tudors to the Victorians. In modern times, we saw the rise of the music halls. That was when popular music really took off in Leicester. Music was always part of big public celebrations. It was also part of daily life in churches and pubs. Nearly all members of the community would hear some sort of live music, on a regular basis.

There is a continuity in musical traditions. Just as church music influenced classical, and secular music became folk, so too, popular music traces its roots back to the days of the Victorian music halls. The arrival of music from other cultures, predominantly jazz in the 1940s and 1950s, and more recently Indian music, has had a marked influence on musical styles and the tastes of the local community.

Why music is important

If you want to understand a community, I once wrote, find out what music its people listened to. Plotting the course of musical history has never been easy. Even when people kept written records and when we had printed newspapers and magazines, music was often neglected unless it was seen to be newsworthy.

Today, it is even harder to keep track of popular music, simply because it is so volatile. Since the rise of the Internet, and, in particular, social media, keeping track of what has been going on has become more difficult. The ten years studied in this article were chosen because I kept detailed records of what I saw, heard and went to. During that decade, bands and artists made use of MySpace (a forerunner of Facebook.) All of what they wrote and uploaded has now disappeared from that platform.

Popular music events do not always leave behind documentary evidence, such as programmes and tickets. These are rare for small gigs in small venues. You pay to get in and the most you get is a stamp on one of your hands. Programmes are only for big concerts at places like the De Montfort Hall. Or concerts of classical music. Once the gig in the small venue had finished and the audience had gone home, nothing was left as evidence that it took place. Unless, someone like me, was there with a notebook and pen, writing down details of what happened. And taking photos.

Music evaporates

Thousands of photos, videos and comments are now put on Facebook every week to mark what gigs people go to. Which bands they have seen. What they thought about them. This material is short-lived. Eventually, it evaporates and is lost. Social historians will not be able to go back to social media, in decades to come, and see what musical life was like, in Leicester, unless someone keeps an account of it now - as it happens. Musical life is something that needs to be preserved. What this decade taught me, is that Leicester is a fantastic place for music. I wrote an article once with the title 'Leicester - the indie capital of the UK.' In it, I claimed that our city outstripped most others for its bands and its music. My aim was to establish Leicester as a city with a proud tradition of music, going back for centuries. If you really want to understand our city, you must understand its music.

JENNY DRURY
*Mum of two who loves writing poetry, usually concerning issues she cares
deeply about. Born in Leicester and developed a love of history during her
school days, just feet from the remains of a medieval king! Studied history at
University, but came back and loves the city, people and sport!*

LOOKING FOR LEICESTER

North of Northampton, South East of Leeds,
as far from the sea as you're able to be,
just off the M1 and the M69,
an hour from London by Midland Main Line.

Meet at the Clock Tower, head down the King Power,
Grace Road for cricket with Aggers and Gower,
the old Granby Halls, the Leicester Riders,
Champions of Europe - the Leicester Tigers.
Tikka masalas, chips, biryanis,
ice cream shakes at Brucciani's,
"guwin up tahn?" "ay up me duck!"
day trips to Skeggy (despite Thomas Cook).

Gujarati and English, Urdu, Somali,
Arabic, Polish, Bengali, Punjabi,
culturally rich, diverse population,
Ugandans, Somalis, mass immigration.
Battle of Bosworth, Richard III,
King in a car park, bones re-interred,
textiles, Topps Tiles, shoes, boots and knitters,
Walkers Crisps, Everards bitters.
Glacier mints, Mastermind games,
Cardinal Wolsey's mortal remains.
Fenwicks, Next and Morgan Squires,
St Martins, High Street and The Shires,
New Walk, Charles Street, Gallowtree Gate,
Beaumont Leys, St Matthew's Estate,
Simpkin & James, British Shoe Corporation,
first BBC local radio station.

Kirby and West – the doorstop dairy,
Schmeichel and Vardy, Claudio Ranieri,
Premier League Champions 2016,
5000-1, miracle team,
three League Cups, four wins at Wembley,
Lineker, Shilton, Pyatt and Selby,
Gordon Banks, Willie Thorne,
Attenborough brothers, all Leicester born,
Mrs Mole and her teenage son Adrian,
Englebert Humperdinck, "Fire" from Kasabian.

Roman ruins, historic sites,
cathedral, mosques, Diwali lights.
LOROS, Corah's, Waterloo Way,
Twycross, Highcross, Lady Jane Grey.
Bradgate Park and Foxton Locks,
Golden Mile, Midland Fox.
Abbey Park, the Jewry Wall,
market stalls, De Montfort Hall.
Semper Eadem, lions on a crest,
I've found my Leicester - and here I will rest.

SIOBHAN LOGAN

*Logan's poetry & non-fiction collections published by Original Plus Press.
Teaches Creative Writing at De Montfort University and co-manages Space Cat
Press. Latest book Desert Moonfire: The Men Who Raced to Space; published
September 2019. https://spacecatpress.co.uk*

OBITUARY FOR THE GRAND UNION CANAL

It was a nesting place
between towpath reeds
for a late brood
of nine ducklings,
looking startled by
the traffic of boots
buggies and bikes.

It was a motorway
for the downsized –
slow–down, go-back
mode of transport;
the oily slide of a
painted boat under
a booming bridge.

It was the resting place
of red-topped lager cans,
a supermarket trolley,
a wind-struck branch,
the door of a Morris Minor,
three frozen chickens
and a blue plastic bag.

It was a museum tour
of textile turrets,
a factory window
bursting with buddleia,
bricks like broken teeth,

still-dripping pipes and
a self-sown sycamore.

It was a filter for
the catch-all of lock walls;
leaf fall and litter,
coot calls and rumours,
condoms and graffiti
and occasionally
bodies.

LAUREN M FOSTER
Is a poet and musician based in Charnwood and a recent graduate of the MA in Creative Writing at the University of Leicester.

BUS STOP, WOODHOUSE EAVES

It's late.
I wait
some more.

This woman comes along,
we've spoke a few times before,
she says 'You'll be lucky.
Took me an hour
to get to Leicester yesterday.
Changed the route again.'
I sigh. We have a brief conversation.
She carries on her walk

This woman comes along,
I've never seen her before,
she looks all colourful in blue
and purple, with a little black
and tan spaniel. She says
'I don't know which way to go.
Cows in one field, sheep in the other.'
She carries on her walk

I take a pen out of my bag,
graffiti the timetable

CAROL LEEMING MBE, FRSA.

Born in Leicester, of parents from Jamaican and Antigua, attended De Montfort University. Carol is a multi-award winning artist in literature, performing arts and digital media. She is a freelance poet, playwright, director and performer. Carol's written, produced and directed drama in Leicester, with work performed nationally in festivals, theatres and BBC Radio.

LOVE THE LIFE YOU LIVE...LIVE THE LIFE YOU LOVE
ABRIDGED CHOREOPOEM

Commissioned by the Centre for New Writing and funded by the AHRC

'Beauty is not in the face, beauty is a light in the heart' Anonymous

Dramatic Monologue
Character:
Martin 24-year-old dual heritage Gay Leicester man works as window dresser

Its 1980's Leicester, the character Martin is conversation with someone and retelling an experience he had on a celebratory night out in St Georges area and Church Cemetery grounds in Leicester

Martin:
1.
I guess this worra lost
then found story,
one yud find tucked away
somewhere you least expect it

2.
1984, it wer warm forra May night
I left haunted fish tank tele home
It wer depressin gale force winds
Crap music loads of boring soaps
Militant miners strike wi bloody Tories
I wer at Helsinki Bar on the lash
Neckin drinks an poppin pills-

Wi mi mates, a right queer lot!
We wer at tha Alternative Miss
Universe a bona big drag fest
I dint enter I'da won wunt ta
I would have liked to any road
Well wunt be fair I am gorgeous eh?

3.
I wer togged up as bizarre pirate
In mi flouncy shirt a black leather
Trousered romantic, wi loads a slap
I wer celebratin myself, big time!
Dancing an snappin to Eurythmics,
I'd gorra new house all paid up
Wot mi real dad had lef it mi
Worra shock, It wer in Highfields
A neat two up two down terrace
Me, Ghetto Queen in the hood
Yeah, I'd give as good as I get

4.
Yuh see I wer adopted baby
Dint know me real dad eh
Or mi real Mam either,
Grew up in St Barnados home
Miles way, up Glenfrith way
Grown up, first time I had jerk
Chicken to eat at carnival I cried
It wer tha bleedin hot wi pepper!
Burra I got to love it, I learnt
How to wine up mi waistline
Like a snake wi reggae soca
Music, I wer gerrin mi culture eh?

5.

Blacks wer on tele nor in Glenfrith
I never saw any black people
Well, the odd one eh? in town,
I wer slagged off in the home
Bullied always, cos I wer black
That's when I started messin
Wi mi foodnor eatin for days
Staff wud send mi to lock up,
I'd bi at window for hours roarin

6.

I felt odd one out to all them
Not just cos a that though
I wer little runt then anyway
Thed mek fun a mi afro hair
I fought I wanted to bi white
I'd dress up in gels clothes
Purra a tee shirt on mi head
Flick it like it wor straight hair

7.

Oh, I blamed mi made up dad
For giving mi away as baby
I thought my mum wer like a
film star, she had to leave mi
that she had *really* loved mi
But mi Dad's lawyer said mi
Real Mam didn't care either
The'd both forgot about mi

8.

Dad: Nathaniel Jacob Lawyer English Jewish
Mam: Lorna Mckinney Nurse Jamaican Christian
Strangers names on paper wer everythin
Cos of their 60's affair I am here,
Lawyer said neither of 'em wanted contact

Dad felt guilty so before he died
He left me tha house on condition
I never ever contact any of his family
I said to the Lawyer well why would I?

9.

He showed mi photo of tha two of em
Together they looked really happy
It weren't a bloody fairy tale worrit?
I'd made up stories about them
Mi whole life, tha truths gutted mi
They wer both bona clever people
I suppose I got somat from 'em both eh?
How I look people get mi all wrong
I might dress dummies inna shop
Now, bur I knew I wer no dummy
I went college I wer good at arts

10.

I 've lost me track now bum!
Oo aah, yeah in Helsinki Bar
Cocktails Long Island Iced Teas
I'm wer at no loss for male company
Bees round honey wi mi love!
Picking up fellas is what I do best
Always they want me to be top
I 'd love to bi bottom forra change
Makes me wonder worr its like
To have it off wi a woman, burra fink
I'd bi dropped like hot cakes by mi friends
I would be wiunt ah! Billy no mates no thanks!

11.

Anyway I cruised the bar wi a big fella
Staggerin we went out for a quickie
Up by tha St Geroges' church ground
He said I looked big, a nice breed

He dint like stuck up Snow queens
Name wot gays call black queens
Who like go out wi white gay men
Cheeky fucker! I said I aint no
Fucking sad snow queen mi oh no!
I 'am an equal opportunities loova!
Specially, if you can flash tha cash
Cos I have got expensive tastes?

12.
Dinge Queens, white gay men
Wi jungle fever for black gay men
Oh they can't ger enuf a mi!
I do look good all 6'3' shaped up
They all have tha same fantasies
I play hot Nubian Prince to their
Shy Princess when wer havin it off
Secretly, I wish I wer bloody princess
Inna way I am, cos I make a big fuss
When they lavish money an gifts on mi
Cos I know they like to be seen wi mi
I am so good looking, I know it
Mi girlfriend well Sheniah mi fag hag
Says finding Mr Right to settle down
To accept mi for all mi kinks
Like mi cross dressing or bein stage performer
Aint bloody easy, so for now it's all about
All the Mr Wrongs... so many men
So little time eh?

13.
Where worra m'duck, ooh aah yes!
Mi an this bloke finished - havin it yuh know
I came out from the bushes
I bumped straight into this other bloke
I reckon he wer watching me ooyah!
You know at it, wi the other bloke

Theres some tha gerr off watchin others
Yuh know, at it, or maybe join in too
Cranin their necks like nosy birds
He were coughin up like car exhaust

14.
I said Oi! Watch it spreadin yer germs
He said, fair Prince I meant not to offend
Only to befriend, in tha manner of tha Greeks
Worra pouncey way a speaking he had
I said have sniff of poppers love, stop
You hacking like a cat wi a fluff ball
He said he'd be alright soon enuf
Fit as a fiddle, as he passed it back
Nor having a sniff, so I did big sniff
Of it, he looked Italian bur he weren't

15.
Suddenly mi guts twisted mi up
Knotted tighter than gnats tweeter
I remembered I aint eaten propley
Well for several days, as is my way
Just loads of booze fags an pills
He said yuh look green around tha gills
Mi spasms rocked mi an he offered
Me a hipflask of rum I drank greedily
Thinkin he talks proper ol 'school
He looked proper vintage as well all
Greeney yellow tweeds, brogue shoes
Big fat moustache wi bushy side burns

16.
Hoverin over me like he wer gon
Kiss me or somat he said all lechy
I see a tot of firewater
Has stiffened you up ol boy!
I just looked at him, as if to say

No chance mate, yur not mi fancy
He blushed faintly an turned away
He looked about 30 ish butch
Broad shouldered an upright
Smiling wi brown eyes an pink
Full lips peepin from his moustache
Wi a severe short back an sides
Dark brown hair slightly wavy on top
He looked at mi again an we both smiled

17

Then two townie gels bumbled along
All white stilettos backcombed up do's
Neckin a bottle a vodka an faggin it
Singin silly song from film Grease
Yur tha one that I want oh oo oo ooo
Their tongues an heels all clackin
One goes forra quick slash in bushes
When she comes back she sees mi
Gigglin, her an her mate eye mi right up
It's as if this other bloke wern't even there
He makes like hes shooin 'em away
As they pass by mi, I give em a wink

18

Ooyah date! this bloke so loses it
Shoutin Fiibertigibbits, harridans whores
Fish dressed up, in cheap bits of skirt!
Heartless harlots, tarty slutty slags
Top of his voice, wi his eyes all bulgin
Bits of spit at tha corners of his gob
Gels walk on like they never heard him
I said wot, them girls are works of fine art
He said, all women were vile harpies
Tha ruin of men drainin their essence
Look at Samson Delilah Caesar Cleopatra
He stood there lookin around then said

By the way, Sidney George Bradshaw is my name
I have not had the pleasure …
His eyes twinkled as he put his hand out
Pleasure, I said, not yet you've not cheeky bugger
Well! talk about in like Flynn!
Martin's my name unless I 'am dragged up
Then I am Maz the Maneater m'duck eh?

CLARE MORRIS

Leicester is a city Clare keeps coming back to. She lived and worked here in the 1980s before eventually working abroad for a number of years. Living in the East Midlands again now, she is sure it won't be long before she's back in Leicester once more.

LISTEN, LET ME TELL YOU ABOUT LEICESTER

And I'll tell you about our loyalty
With our hopeful matchday scarves hoisted high
In swathes of blue and white or green and red
As Foxes and Tigers prowl -
And our all-weather archaeologists digging deep in a cheerless carpark,
On knees, before our longed-for king -

And I'll tell you about our literature
And that ruffian Joe waiting to entertain us on the stair with Mr Sloane
And Sue with her fractions and her secrets
And their word-wit that sparkles in unlikely places -

And I'll tell you about our language
As we go down paggy sarvo wi' Tezza, Bezza an' Shazza
An' if you tell us oo waree wi' en we might let you come along too, duck -

And I'll tell you about our light
And our streetlamps, Diwali-dreaming,
Alive with sudden illumination, warm as egg yolks,
As they pool their wares in Sainsbury's puddles
Waiting for another Melton Road dawn -

And I'll tell you about our love
And our Saturday-night serenading at the Palais de Danse
Where Mum met Dad
And knew that she'd found
Home.

SARAH KIRBY
THE GUILDHALL

EMMA LEE
UNTOWERED

Lord Mayor's Parlour, The Guildhall, Leicester

Shakespeare once walked past the door I walk through
on his way to the stage with his band of players.

On an October evening, forty red plush chairs held people.

Once, only men stood here, in sight of the Guildsmen's
Host and Chalice emblem, governing the city I call home.

I, a woman, stood in front of the fireplace.

A mother hurries two children into the Great Hall,
hoping for a breather before home and repeats of *Tangled*.

It wasn't shyness or faulty hearing that had muted me.

A gaggle of students skip past to giggle at the prison cells,
hoping to catch a glimpse of the grey lady in the library.

Unlike Rapunzel, I made my own escape.

The Earl of Huntington's portrait retains its ghostly legs.
He looks bored as if passion might be below his dignity.

My voice is finally ready. I can read without shame.

The Lord Mayor's chair is out of bounds.
I am unencumbered by the weight of office,

the restrictions of a tower. I am free to speak.

ISABELLA WHY

Is a keen writer of poetry, short stories, and non-fiction. Her love of writing has developed out of her fascination of different cultures and customs. Isabella has a BA degree in Anthropology and Archaeology from Durham University and has had work published in Forward Poetry.

A BEAUTIFUL BLEND

Our city is old.
She's seen many a sunrise
And fall.

She has sheltered Celtic clans
When iron ruled the world.
She heard the tribal call of Britons
And watched their rituals and their arrows fly.

The Romans took the city next
And gave her their famous baths.
Then Mercia claimed her,
Later the Vikings had their say.

She found her way into William
The Conqueror's
Doomsday book.

She watched the tale of Lear,
Cordelia, Regan and Goneril
Before Shakespeare wrote his play.

John of Gaunt built her
A grand church
To protect the Crown of Thrones
And worship the king of kings.

She strongly stood throughout the War
Of the Roses,
And is the eternal home
Of King Richard lll.

She was swamped by Tudors
Lady Jane Grey, Robert Dudley
And Cardinal Wolsey.
All came her way.

When the Civil War arrived
She became a Roundhead
And rejoiced on victory day.

With clothes and shells
She provided for the First World War
And was decorated,

With the Arch of Remembrance
Now she is a sea of faces
And a beautiful blend of cultures
That is ever full of wonders.

JEMIMA CHILDS

A 22 year old poet and journalist living in London. She's been writing since she was twelve, and enjoys the creative process of forming a poem.
She is Foyle Young Poet, Times Young Poet and Ted Hughes Young Poet, and has been published in the anthology 'Flowers from the Dark'.

GRANNY SMITH

You bought me apples from Leicester market
And I pretended I was a horse,
Nibbling them from your open palm then
Galloping off as you stroked my baby curls

The sweet juice dripped down my chin
As I tried to munch the nutty seeds,
You told me I'd better not eat any soil
Or an apple tree might grow inside my tummy

I rubbed my sticky fingers through the grass in Abbey Park
Then we sprinkled the seeds like the freckles on our noses
We took the bus back along Melton Road:
I sat in your lap and you sang until I slept

Now, when I hear the stir of the wind through the city's oaks
I feel the tug of their roots grounding me

LAUREN M FOSTER
THE ANGEL OF WELFORD ROAD

On nights like this you see her,
if you peer into the shadows,
forever searching,
wings aquiver
as her little torso quakes
with tears she cannot make.

Past the cenotaph she goes,
past the names of the fallen,
all along the moonlit path
through holly, beech and yew.
Moonbeams fall on ambers
and russets juxtaposed
with faded plastic Poundland flowers

on nights like this. You see her
if you peer into the shadows,
forever searching every cranny,
every nook, arms beseeching
badger, muntjac, rat and fox.
Her little hand still carries
the posy of roses they buried with her.

On nights like this you see her.
If you peer into the shadows
you might find her head,
alas, kicked off in '76
by boisterous youths with nothing to do.
They played catch for a while
until one nearly got knocked out,
so they threw it

over the hedge,
onto the railway sidings
where it lies to this day,
nestled in a bed
of bay-willow herb and ragwort.

On nights like this you see her,
if you peer into the shadows.

RESHMA MADHI

Has had poetry published in Ugly Tree Zine and more recently, Art Ascent magazine. Reshma has worked in publishing and communications and continues to be a feature writer for online lifestyle magazines. She has strong links to Leicester through family; being a first home in the UK for her parents.

A CITY I SHOULD BELONG TO

I could have been born there
Or at least grew up there
Or went to uni there
Got married there
Could still settle down there now

My parents must have been living not far when they first arrived separately
To me it was just this distant, other place I visited perhaps once every five years
For a wedding or a funeral, to pick up a relative visiting from abroad
Doing their UK tour of all the key stops…
Wembley, Finchley, Leicester, Walsall, Coventry, Bradford, Preston.

I remember once we were on our way back home, squeezed into one car
And we had to turn into this side street,
It was like every other in this part of the UK world
Tiny, narrow, terraced houses, all identical.
I felt like I was on set in some British film, something set in some kind of
industrial old world town
Dad spoke out, he said he lived here once, when he first arrived.
It could have been my home here too.
I would have blended in. How strange I felt like an oddity.
Right here, walking through the park, there must have been dozens of us, settled
over various years.
Spot the white person, my brothers joked.

Round the corner, the shops parade the latest fashions.
I try to keep up with whatever colours or styles are in now.
We all know the spot to get the best chevro or mithai
I remembered then I was exactly here years ago.

We'd made a rare pilgrimage to see a proper New Year Festival
With music, and rowdiness, fireworks set off in the road, people milling about.
There's no closed doors or not talking or knowing who your neighbours are
Or who everyone is.

Everyone watches you when you arrive. They know you are a visitor, a stranger.
Nothing gets missed when you live so close together. No secrets here.
But even those grown up here, themselves children of migrants
Feel it's changed too much now. Even they wonder if the change is too quick
Now perhaps their neighbours have formed their own communities and walls,
Even though they are right next door.

I could blend in too, much more than where I grew up down South
I could belong here too, it's almost a home.
I want to be from these parts because it's got the food I love and the community
I crave
That knowing, it's not just the obvious like my accent or getting lost walking
the streets.
Somehow, it's known I don't come from round here
Something sets me apart from Leicester
It's just a city we almost all belong to

JENNY DRURY
IMAGINE

Imagine a city that race can't divide
where black, white and Asian thrive side by side,
sharing their schools, their shops and their teams,
their workplaces, their restaurants, their family dreams.

Imagine a city where history calls
from ramparts, and ruins and old Roman walls,
telling of queens and their ill-fated claims,
protecting with pride a dead king's remains.

Imagine a city ignoring a tide
of critics and doubters - expectations defied,
where teams can unite and together achieve
remarkably more than they'd ever believed!

Imagine a city, leading the way
in showcasing space and our own DNA,
whose factories have fed us and kept us well dressed,
whose artists inspire us and theatres impress.

Imagine a city whose sons and whose daughters
have thrilled us, amused us, and recently taught us
to conserve our planet, stirring the nation
to care for our world for the next generation.

No need to imagine,
step right inside -
Leicester will greet you
with joy and with pride.

JULIE GARDNER

Julie Gardner taught in primary schools for over forty years. She is currently studying for an MA in Creative Writing at Nottingham Trent University. She lived and taught in Leicestershire for many years but now lives in Nottingham.

FIRST GRANDCHILD

A body on the line, near Bedford
delayed my train.
I stood on Leicester station as that news
subdued the waiting throng, heard murmurs
of regret, irritation.
For me, the day brought long awaited
news of birth, while on that railway track
a life had ended.

Today, I wait again,
for a train that runs on time.
Now, as then,
I wish for you a life fulfilled,
love, excitement, laughter, friends,
the unsung luxury of hopefulness.

SARAH PERSSON

Born in Leicester in 1982. She moved away aged 18 to study English at the University of Southampton, travelled for a few years and then trained to become a teacher. Sarah lives in South Wales, by the sea enjoying the chaos of two children, a pug and a lovely husband.

MEMORIES OF ROSSA'S DONUT STALL, LEICESTER MARKET, CIRCA 1987

Daddy, do you remember the donuts in the market?
Your hand at my shoulder in the queue.
Pallid dollops crackled one by one in hot golden oil
Delivering a Saturday sermon:
Like the Pied Piper calling children.

Daddy, do you remember it was always freezing waiting for our donuts?
I leaned into your leg. Brown nylon, too thin for this wind.
I looked up at the metal conveyor. Plump, golden, hot:
One by one, our donuts tumbled into a pit of sugar
Twenneh tomatus ferra paand.
A swell of diamond dust.

Daddy, do you remember the wooden donut stick?
The man lifted and twirled each donut, like he was a conductor.
Your hand in your pocket: 20 pence each.
More sugar I would hope.
He flicks both donuts into a white paper bag
Rolls down the top. I couldn't tell you anything about his face.
Just that the donuts, they were ours...

Thanks Daddy!
You pinched out each one in squares of tissue paper,
It was like the loo roll in public toilets.
The donut burned through the paper.
Made its own mist.
My short cold fingers danced:
Moved left and right to find a cool spot to hold.
Blow! Blow!
Then I was just yours.

SARAH KIRBY
LEICESTER MARKET

FOQIA HAYEE

From Amritsar, Foqia's been writing poems and stories since she was a teenager. She holds a Masters in Graphic Design from Punjab University. Her play "Match me if you can" was staged at Rudolf Steiner London in 2009. Moved to Leicester in 2013 where she continues to write on impulse.

UPLANDS PARK

Have you heard of this fresh air treatment?
You could be one of the recipients
Only if you dedicate
A time to be fit and appreciate
A walk in Uplands Park
Preferably during light hours, avoid the dark
This park is so anti-pollution
A walk in there is the solution
To most problems that you might face
Stress, frustration, regrets you chase
Till they disappear in the air.
Have you heard of this fresh air treatment?
It's free with no obligation
As you step in
You are surrounded by this invisible friend
With whom you quickly blend
You get treated as if you are the only one there
Worries, anxieties, you share
Walk, jog, fast or slow
at your pace, just let go
To others, say hello, morning or just ignore
No one will mind, as they too, know the score.
Have you heard of this fresh air treatment?
Be warned it could become an addiction
You can explore further with no restriction
Go on outside exercise machines
To get a flavour of different routine
There is a playground with swings
So kids you can bring

Dogs, running around, to some, might be a concern
Do not reject, as soon you will learn
They are controlled, free to run around,
But by master's voice, still bound.
Have you heard of this fresh air treatment?
There are benches to sit and rest
In case of rain shelters you can suggest
It shouldn't be hard to install
Toilets! Suggested by all
CCTV, written rules, hotline for users
Could be in place, to avoid abusers

How many miles we cover?
It would be good to discover
There are endless benefits, of that you can be sure
This friendly air is the cure
Uplands Park is waiting
So, start dating

ALUN ROBERT

Is a prolific creator of lyrical verse. His poems have achieved success in poetry competitions and featured in literary magazines, anthologies and on the web.

LATE AFTERNOON IN LEICESTER

Darkness pervades.
Leicester enchanting.
Street lights turned on, augmented
by big stores next door
to those boarded up, closed. The

guy standing next me
closely inspects his faux Rolex.
Bit like my pseudo Timex
if only I could read it but
my specs are steamed up. We've

been waiting for ages,
an 86 long overdue, rain
dribbling inside his collar en route
down his spine to the coccyx.
Just like me. For

I smile; he does too.
We both shake our heads as
water flies from my flat cap
like a greyhound off trap while
his turban is more dignified. Though

we moan about the weather,
we talk about Tigers,
They're not the team they once were,
I concur with a furled brow for
we'd seen them lose. Today

no sign of a delayed 86
with both of us starving, so
we set off for an Italian;
he likes penne pasta while
I adore margheritas. We

both went to City of Leicester
(I was a year younger)
each had a gap year grafting
long hours in Highcross.
Hardly high wages. But

we're now both at uni:
him Leicester me De Montfort
both aiming for a 2.1 (at least)
to keep our parents happy,
to keep job prospects alive. Back

at the stop an 86 arrives
packed to the brim with
seats taken by the grey youth
as the elderly stand clutching
shopping and purses. Then

we alight at the same stop,
shaking hands departing.
Different yet brothers;
both sons of Leicester,
both with hearts in our City.

DR ROGER CRAIK

Born in Leicester. He now lives in America. His poems have been published in England, Australia and America, Bulgaria, Romania, and Belarus. He has written four books of poetry, the most recent is Down Stranger Roads (2014). Writing poetry is now all that matters, and remembering Leicester matters too.

HOME (1956-65)

I

The rainy fields
of sheep and cows in Leicestershire.

The Morris Minor
ambling the narrow roads and lanes.

And at the front my parents,
young in their coats.

II

Every road
led out of Leicester into Leicestershire.
Peatling Magna, Peatling Parva, Wistow Hall,

Leicestershire moving in the small
triangular window.

BERNADETTE LOUGHRAN.

Was born, educated and lives in Leicester. Being land-locked Bernadette has a fascination for the sea, maritime navigation and wooden sailing ships. Interests include community singing, the arts, architecture and British history. A part-time water colour artist, this is her first venture into painting a picture with words.

LEICESTER, A POEM

This heart of England
beats steady and true.
A smoke free zone.
Clean air not blue.

The Romans came.
They saw. They conquered.
Naming us Ratae.
Their Mosaics recently discovered.
Still used today is their Fosse Way.

Our Castle is no more.
The Great Hall is all that remains.
The Castle wall defended,
during the siege of the Civil War.

Henry VIII at Hampton Court
did summon Cardinal Wolsey.
On route, illness took his life.
He is buried at Leicester Abbey.

Tourism and travel follows the book.
First began by a temperance Thomas Cook.

Our fine Railway Station in London
has not yet been surpassed.
Rescued by campaigners like Sir John Betjeman,
statuesque at St Pancras.

Industrialisation brought many a trade.
Factory upon Factory grew and grew.
From Boots and Shoes, to Hosiery well made.
Our expertise still needed in Engineering,
Health and Science, to name but a few.

Kings and Queens have courtly passed.
One remained after Battle lost.
His Crown dislodged, this Son of York.
His bones discovered beneath a Car Park.

King Richard III, World status has he.
Ignominiously interred at Grey Friars.
Ceremoniously reburied in the Cathedral he lies.
Entombed, honoured, dignified.

Worldly battles fought The 17th Regiment of Foot.
Renamed The Leicestershire Regiment.
'Hindoostan' on their Cap Badge.
Name upon name that gave up their lives.
We must ensure they are never forgot.

Our City is rich in history, culture and pride.
World nationalities live and work side by side.
Premier prowess in Sport across the board.
Basketball, Cricket, Rugby and Football.

Our emblem, a central Cinque Foil.
A Wyvern above and a Motto below:
'Semper Eadem' - Always the Same.
No need to boast. We know who we are.
Come visit our City, UK and afar.

MARIANNE WHITING

Arrived from Sweden in 1973. She completed her MA but missed the boat home.
She is still married to the reason for her poor time-keeping. When Marianne
retired, she indulged her passion for writing. Her Shieldmaiden Trilogy is
published by Accent Press, other writing has appeared in magazines and
anthologies.

EXCERPT FROM TO SAVE A KINGDOM,

... Drunk with victory, weighed down with booty our army made its way to
Leicester. Without Ragnwald, Prince Rhun and their warriors there were not
enough men to leave a force at Tamworth but the raid would serve as a
bargaining point with King Edmund. Much of the way to Leicester we followed
Watling Street which supposedly made up the boundary between Mercia and
the Danelaw. It was well travelled, not least by successive armies fighting each
other for supremacy of the Five Boroughs. It took us less than a day to get to
Leicester. At dusk we saw the town walls. These had once been strong, built of
granite. Now I saw a patchwork of repairs in brick and wood. People were at
work there. Lines of men and women carried buckets of earth to build up the
ramparts and carts brought rocks to strengthen the brickwork. They withdrew to
the shelter of the walls when they saw us. I wondered why as in order to enter
this borough we would have to cross a river which flowed in several different
channels creating islands connected to each other and the town by bridges. Only
one bridge led to the city-gate and it was long and exposed. It seemed to me
impossible to take this borough by storm. We pitched tents and built shelters a
couple of furlongs away from the town walls. That night we posted lookouts but
saw little activity on the town walls.

The next morning Wulfstan accompanied only by Cuaran, King of Jorvik
and the most important chieftains with their hirds, rode up to the bridge.
Wulfstan was, unusually, dressed in bishops' garb. A white, gold-embroidered
robe with wide sleeves, covered by a cape in deepest purple, held together by a
magnificently bejewelled brooch. He carried a mitre and his freshly shaved
tonsure looked pale in the sunlight. Cuaran stayed a few paces behind.
Wulfstan's servant blew a horn to announce their arrival. A couple of guards
peered over the ramparts. They vanished and soon returned to open the heavy
wooden gates. The reeve appeared. He was accompanied by a priest in faded
vestments. Both welcomed Wulfstan with a great show of respect, the priest

knelt and kissed Wulfstan's ring and so did the reeve. The reeve then bent his knee to Cuaran as well. Perhaps he had decided to accept the inevitable or maybe the town truly preferred a Norse to a Saxon king, it wasn't always easy to tell in these borderlands where fighting was almost constant and the population held as many Danes as Anglians and Britons.

Word went out that there was to be no looting here. Our army had done well at Tamworth and all seemed content to return to camp and make themselves comfortable while Cuaran and Wulfstan were conducted into the town by the reeve. They were followed by their hirds, the most important of the chieftains and by me trying to keep out of sight. The guards saluted, ox-carts, pack-horses and people laden with goods made room for us to pass. Many made the sign of the cross when the Archbishop rode past, some fell to their knees. Wulfstan made the sign of blessing over the bystanders left and right. They seemed to know who he was, or at least what he was. I wondered what they really thought of this warrior-priest, entering their town at the head of an army.

I was reminded that it was only a couple of years ago that the previous King of Jorvik had gained the borough. Houses still showed charred timbers and fresh repairs to thatch and wattle and daub walls. Away from the one main street it could have been a village with cultivated fields and animals grazing among patches of wasteland. The reeve led us to a small church. It was built in stone with one end using the tall remains of a Roman building that must, long ago, have been very grand. The church was surrounded by wooden houses one of which could be described as a hall but hardly the abode of a king or bishop. The yard in front was busy, servants and guards fetching and carrying or just standing around talking. Our horses, impatient as they sensed water, feed and rest, stamped their hooves and snorted. Dogs woke from their slumber, sniffed and barked at the newcomers. Whips cracked and shouts echoed until order was restored. The chieftains followed Wulfstan towards the hall. I tried to join them but Wulfstan spoke to a servant who approached me.

"Mistress Sigrid, I have been told to take you to suitable accommodation for you and your women servants."

I wondered where Wulfstan had decided was a suitable place for me and my women warriors. It turned out to be a religious community, three small wooden houses clustered around a stone cross. I was received in an austere room where the only light came from a single flickering tallow next to a crucifix on a small table. A tight-lipped Abbess surveyed my blood-splattered tunic, my trews and my weapons.

"I am told you are of royal blood," she said. "I am of course honoured that Archbishop Wulfstan has chosen my house to receive you and your servant women."

We looked at each other in a silence poised somewhere between uncomfortable and hostile. Then she resumed:

"Of course I shall be able to find somewhere to dispose of your weapons and I'm sure I can provide you with a dress."

"I am Sigrid Kveldulfs daughter. I am a warrior with my own followers, both women and men. They all remain with me as do my weapons. As for my clothes, they are well suited to my cause and I see no reason to change. I thank you for your offer of hospitality but I shall not need to inconvenience you."

She glared at me and the wrinkles round her thin, disapproving mouth deepened as she bade me farewell.

I crossed the bridge and joined the rest of the Cumbrians on the other side of the river. Our tents made a small settlement where warriors and camp followers gathered around the cooking fires. I claimed a space for me and my hird. A couple of thralls took the horses to find grazing. The camp grew as stragglers caught up but one important person was still missing. Nobody knew what had happened to Kjeld Gunnarson. I didn't quite dare think that he had perished. I saw none of his men but there again I didn't know all of them so I could be wrong. We settled down to the daily routine of foraging for food, cooking, weapons practice and games. I found it utterly tedious.

One market day I took my women to visit the town. They deserved some distraction from the routine of the camp. I also thought they were, like me, homesick. We all had items from the looting of Tamworth that we wanted to barter for more useful things. I told Kveldulf he could come and the men also joined us under various pretexts. I thought for a moment that they lacked confidence in my ability to keep the girls safe. But no sooner had we entered the city before Thorfinn made a lame excuse to visit the area along the river where some of the local women made themselves available. He was followed by Varg. Both had a spring in their step as they made their way along the rows of houses.

"Can I go with them?" said Kveldulf and Anlaf laughed.

"No, I think they have business of their own," he said, "men's business."

"Why aren't you going with them then?"

"I thought I'd, have a look around."

Anlaf stayed with us as we walked from stall to stall admiring jewellery made from bone, ivory from the South, jet from Whitby, amber from the Baltic and intricate filigree silver brooches and pendants. Unn found a scabbard inlaid with silver for her knife, we all bought new kerchiefs to stop our leather jerkins chafing against our necks. Hildur found a pair of boots and declared her old ones beyond repair. Ylva admired a comb made of bone with animal figures carved on it. She decided it was just the thing to tame her unruly mane.

"And what about you?"

Ylva teased Anlaf. He blushed and dropped the string of beads he'd been looking at. Now, that's enough, I thought. Keeping a wench at the camp was one thing, presumably he paid for her services but buying her presents was going too far.

"Yes, Gyda would like that, why don't you buy it for her?"

"Yes, yes, of course," he mumbled.

I was struck by the look on his face. Confusion, guilt, resentment, poor Anlaf, bound by oath to a chieftain who was also his sister-in-law. Would Ragnar have been more understanding? What did Ragnar...? Feeling my temper rising I decided that line of thought would lead me nowhere. It had to be enough that on Buttermere farm the only children who bore any resemblance to Ragnar were mine. I took a couple of deep breaths and joined the girls by a wood-turner's hut. I felt a tug at the sight of small toys, a horse on wheels, a spinning top. Kveldulf stared at them.

"Well, of course I'm too old for that sort of thing," he said, "but we could get something for Harald."

"Yes, and you could pla... ah... look after them until we get home."

It was all very well for Ragnar to tell me not to think of home or of Harald but how could I not?

The market was busy and we grew tired of jostling with people. I decided we needed food and drink. The one tavern was full and we had to make do with places along a trestle table outside a small hut where a widow dressed in an apron that may once have been white made good profit from visitors to the market. I ordered meat and ale from the old crone. The ale was watery and the meat tough but a fire burned close by and made it feel tolerably warm.

"I promise never to complain about the food at home again," said Ylva as she shifted a mouthful to chew on the other side.

We had a fine view of the comings and goings along one of the main routes through town. Just watching the people milling about was exciting and the girls kept a running commentary on what they saw. But they fell silent and stared round-eyed when a couple of King Anlaf Cuaran's guards made room for a young girl to have sole access to the stall selling used clothes. She couldn't have been much older than Kveldulf but her bearing spoke of privilege far beyond anything he could ever hope for. Her dress had once been fine enough for a queen but the velvet was torn and the embroidery frayed and the dirt from the journey from Tamworth too ingrained to be shifted. I had heard about this girl, a hostage called Wulfrun, taken to be used as a bargaining point with Edmund.

She looked pale and gaunt; the round cheeks of maidenhood had melted away revealing a pair of high cheekbones. But there was about her a quiet confidence as she rejected one garment after another to the consternation of the stallholder. Next to her, politely ignored by the girl, stood the Abbess, her lips getting thinner every time her suggestions were turned down. I almost laughed when I thought that the Abbess had her work cut out with this self-possessed child.

Occupied with Wulfrun and her shopping my companions didn't notice when I choked on my ale. I had to blink to make sure my eyes weren't playing tricks on me. Grim I might have missed despite his limp but Olvir I'd know anywhere in whatever disguise. As they passed us, I thought they increased their pace.

"Don't ask," I said to Anlaf, "don't draw attention to us. I'll see you back at the camp."

Anlaf shushed Hildur and raised his eyebrows at me. I shook my head, put some hack-silver on the table and rose to follow the pair. Olvir turned a corner by a bone-workers shop and I followed.

Grim and Olvir weaved their way past workshops and stalls. It was hard to keep them in view while dodging people and animals in the crowded street. I cursed as I stepped in a fresh dog turd. I gagged on the stench but kept my eye on Olvir. They had slowed down again and walked without hurry, a monk and a young novice. There was nothing remarkable about them. I had expected them to head for Wulfstan at the hall but they turned in the opposite direction and made their way along a heavily rutted lane. It led away from the market and the main street. I had no idea where I was. A woman swore at me when I bumped into her pig. The animal ran squealing down the street and ran into a man. He kicked it into the path of another man who lost his balance. He dropped a tray full of pots and the crash as it hit the ground mixed with the pig's squealing and the shouting and laughter of the onlookers. The woman chasing her pig shouted as she passed:

"May you join Loki under the serpent, you miscreant. Go back to the trolls where you belong."

The unlucky potter tried to pick his wares out of the dust and filth but came up with nothing but cracked and broken pieces. He rose and towering above me, shook his fist in my face.

"Bloody hussy," he growled, "that's two whole days' work. Look at them, broken everyone, you cursed child of Satan. What are you going to do about this? I can't sell shards at the market. You Devil's spawn. How will I feed my children?"

While abusing me in ever more colourful language he looked at me assessing how much I could be expected to pay him in compensation. People gathered closer. Some seemed inclined to join in so I hastened to offer the potter a piece of hack-silver. As I expected he looked at it with scorn.

"Two days" work!" he growled.

I added a small coin. He continued to scowl but when I swept my cloak back, he saw my sword and took the silver. Behind him I saw Olvir's wide-eyed, over-the-shoulder look, as he hurried away from me. I retreated from the small crowd and walked in his direction. Nobody followed, as far as I could see. I walked quickly until I reached the corner where Olvir had disappeared. It was too late. Olvir and Grim were gone.

I looked around me. Where was I? I had no desire to retrace my steps and face the crowd I'd left behind so I continued walking. Here were no streets only trampled paths between houses and shacks surrounded by gardens and small fields. Pigs, chickens and cows were kept behind rough fences. The houses were small with workshops and stores inside, cooking fires and privies outside, the air full of smells, most of them unpleasant. People looked away as I passed but I could feel their eyes on my back. The houses gave way to shrub-covered wasteland. I soon reached the town-wall and came to a halt. The sun was in its afternoon descent, south-west. That didn't help me much as I didn't know which direction I had started from.

"We seem to have lost them."

It was no more than a whisper. I gasped. A hand covered my mouth. A cloak wound around me and pressed my body close to that of another. How could I have been so careless? Intent on following I hadn't noticed that I was myself a prey. I didn't know the voice in my ear.

"Don't scream. We should talk you and I, Mistress Sigrid."

I relaxed my stance. The man let go. I spun away and drew my knife. I stood face to face with a stranger. He was dressed as a merchant but, despite his short stature and slightly crooked back, there was more than a hint of the warrior about him. He stepped back and grinned.

"You won't need your knife," he said, "you are perfectly safe with me. Ragnar Sweinson's sword demands too much respect for me to impose myself on his wife. Besides you still have your own sword to defend your honour."

He giggled as he removed not only his fur hat but the black plaits and the long fringe that were attached to it. I stared at Anlaf Sithricson, the man we all called Cuaran, King of Jorvik. He was younger than he had seemed at a distance, younger than my score and one, yet he was a battle-hardened warrior and a king. Not that there was much royalty about him now as he laughed and slapped his thigh.

"Please don't bother to curtsy," he said. "It's a good disguise, isn't it?" Then his mood changed.

"Mistress Sigrid, you have caused me some inconvenience today. The two men you followed were my messengers. I do need to speak with them but the commotion you caused made this impossible. I take it they are familiar to you."

I didn't know whether to trust this king who used messengers so secret he couldn't meet them in his own hall. On the other hand I couldn't refuse to answer.

"I thought the boy looked like my fostring. I may have been mistaken."

"Not sure? And yet you were very determined in your pursuit of them. Who sent you to look out for them?"

"What? Nobody sent me, what do you mean? What's happening? What's Olvir doing?"

I had raised my voice. He shushed me and looked in all directions.

"Mistress Sigrid, you need to keep your voice down. So, Wulfstan's little spy is your fostring, is he? Interesting."

"Olvir was taken on by the Archbishop as apprentice scribe."
I seethed but managed to keep my voice steady.

"The difference is sometimes not obvious," said Cuaran. "The boy is good, he has a talent for finding out things, information, details about people."

"I shall speak to the Archbishop. He has no right to put the boy at risk. Olvir could be killed and I … and I…"

Cuaran, hard-faced, stared at me, the whites of his eyes had a bluish tint. It unsettled me making my voice fade to a whisper. He shook his head.

"No, running to Wulfstan won't do you any good. You must accept that we all have a part to play in this. I shall fulfil my destiny as the Norns have woven it for me since I was born and so shall the rest of you. The boy, you, Wulfstan, all of us."

The light-hearted note was gone from his voice. A dagger at my throat could not have made his point more clearly. We stood in silence.

"Am I free to leave, Sire?"

He seemed to have forgotten about me and nodded. Then as an afterthought he said:

"You will stay away from my messengers, whatever they are to you. And you are not to mention to Wulfstan that they report to me. You are not to interfere; it would spell misfortune for you and yours. I hope you understand that. Yes, you may go."

Extract permission courtesy of Accent Press ISBN for To Save a Kingdom ISBN 9781786153654, eISBN 9781786153005

SHIRLEY FIFIELD

Leicester born. Her parents are of the Windrush generation. She and her twin were the first black kids at Linden Junior. On leaving they were awarded books. Shirley for coming out of her shell. She's travelled widely and seen the world in Leicester. She's still coming out of her shell.

THE CLOCK TOWER REMAINS

Former buildings have been erased
In their place
Gardens created
Stretching for miles

The Clock Tower remains
Flanked by two lions
A warning to armies of hate
To stay away

Artificial intelligence
Programmed to support
Human Rights

Leicester now one of the
Only settled cities
Where refugees can find welcome

STANLEY IYANU

Is 28 and an amateur writer and poet. He started writing poems at 12 years old and it blossomed into writing stories and songs. He currently works for an insurance company, which is surprisingly interesting and he likes to cook and use self-deprecating humour.

STAYCATION

The best holiday that I have been on so far was a staycation, in England - down in Leicester.
It was a warm day; the sun was out, emblazoned in the sky.
I felt an ease, I felt at ease.
I walked into a coffee shop, sat by an artificial fireplace, underneath chipped red brick hearth and surround. With a cup of hot coffee and a Cheshire cat smile.
Was I alone?
No.
You were where.
Your blue eyes told so much and yet nothing at all. A mystery in front of me. A mystery that captured my attention,
momentarily. When you didn't catch me looking.
I look round and I had crowds around me.
People going about their business and their lives.
Deep into their thoughts and engrossed in their conversations,
their significant others and their life. But-
You were with me.
A peaceful reminder of a home from home,
a faraway destination.
The break I needed and wanted.
In Leicester, where I fell in love.

ELLEN ABDULMUMINOV

Author and teacher who knits, so long as the cat keeps out of the yarn. She wrote Taste of Sarband: Culinary Histories and Dishes of Tajikistan. She considers Tajikistan to be her second home. She is inspired by the natural and cultural beauty of both her homes across the globe.

DEFINED BY MORE THAN ONE PERSON

It is mildly sunny when I meet Susan at Costa for coffee. Mother of my best friend since class five, Jane, Susan had been like a second mother to me. And as is the case with second mothers, they are sometimes even better than first mothers because you don't have to live with them, just get their advice and snacks when you go around for a visit. The latter part is nice. The first part is nice too, because while Susan was sharp witted, she could also be sharp-tongued. Nurturing was not a word to describe her. I could not imagine her as a grandmother.

I always loved Costa Coffee. It wasn't too far from home, so my parents and I would occasionally go there for a snack and hot beverage. Coffee for dad, tea for mom, and usually a hot chocolate for me. I wasn't a big coffee drinker. Mom had tried to get us to go to any of the little independent cafes on Queens Road rather than give the 'big brand' our money, but I was stuck on Costa. At this point, it had become a bit of a tradition. I'd even gone there a couple of times with my boyfriend, Jamal, when we visited my parents on a break from university. I hadn't gone there with Susan before, and it had actually surprised me a bit when she invited me out for a bite without Jane there as well. Then again, my mother had taken Jane out several times to counsel her on school, university choices, and dealing with her younger brothers.

The red exterior of Costa is painted currant, not the colour of natural brick. I swear it has gotten darker, but maybe it is just the clouds. Mildly sunny is, after all, mostly grey. The glass makes the inside look dim, but I see Susan a little ways in against the wall. She is facing away. I go in and head over, peering over her shoulder as I approach.

"Hope you haven't been waiting long."

"A little bit, but only because I was early. How are you doing, dear? Do you want to get something to eat? My treat."

I thank her. For her lack of tenderness, she can be generous, and we go to the counter. It's rather empty, and we are immediately asked what we want.

"Just a refill of hot water for me," Susan responds. "And you?"

"I'll have a…"

I pause. Beyond a hot chocolate, I'm not sure, but I hate making people wait.

"Um…er…I'll…"

Raking my eyes over the glass displays, I quickly choose.

"A teacake."

I don't really want it, but I'm not opposed to it. It's a medium choice. We sit. I nibble on the teacake. Susan drinks her tea. Something doesn't feel right in the air.

"So, what have you been up to lately?" I ask, "I hear John has a big role in his school's play."

"Yeah, he's been going on and on about that," Susan responds.

I continue the small talk as something intuitive prods at my stomach.

"When's the performance? I'm sure we'll want to come and see."

"I'll let your family know when John tells me,"

Susan takes another sip.

"We're all really concerned about you dating Jamal."

For a moment the comment doesn't process, it's spoken so normally.

"Pardon?"

"That's why I wanted to meet with you. We're just all concerned about you."

I know who the we is. It's her whole family, possibly members of mine, too. They had made one-off comments every once in a while, about Jamal. They made it excessively, to the point of suspicion, clear they were never opposed to his brown skin. The fact he was a person of colour wasn't objectionable to them, even if it was a big enough deal to be mentionable in the first place. We'd grown up with enough Indian neighbours and Ugandan schoolmates to be above using race as an objection.

Susan continues. I'm unsure if she's noticed I'm not eating or drinking anymore.

"He's a Muslim. You know they don't believe in the same God that we do."

"Actually we do, they're all Abrahamic religions…"

"I know you think that from things you've read, but it's not the same. We describe our God with love and forgiveness. The Muslim's God punishes people. It's different."

But is it? I'm flooded with memories. Jamal and I met at University and had fallen hard right away. He invited me out on a date within the first week, and soon we were spending most of our days together between our shared courses, date nights, and study breakfasts. Yes, he was Muslim, but in the same way someone is a vegetarian or a Londoner. It affects some of their behaviour but doesn't define their entirety. Susan's always considered me a little progressive, but it still surprises me with the fervour in her voice when she speaks against my statement. I can feel my insides lurch as I try to think of how to even begin to respond.

"Is this what you wanted to meet to talk about? Is this it?"

"I wouldn't minimize it like that,"

Susan makes a tutting sound. I feel myself shrink into myself a little. That's the same noise she makes when she is scolding her youngest son. I've never had it directed at me before, and it's not pleasant. I feel like I'm being treated like a child, someone who doesn't know any better.

"It's something that we need to talk about. We care about you too much to watch you make a mistake."

"So, this is an intervention?"

"No, just me sharing my concerns with you. I mean, what if he tries to control you? If he tries to make you stop working or control who you can see? Those men are like that, you know."

"He would never do that."

My response doesn't even begin to address the wrongness of what she's said. Jamal isn't like that at all. She's known him for a year now, surely, she's seen he's not like that. Beyond that, what made her think it was okay to make that assumption about Muslim men in the first place? Our city is far from homogeneous. How can she have gone this far in life without dispelling that stereotype.

"Jamal is proud of me, just like I'm proud of him. He supports everything I do. He's helping me prepare for an interview next week."

The conversation continues on, but I barely catch the details of Susan's argument. There was something in there about him keeping me from going to church (not that I went regularly anyway), something else about our children, and what would I do if they weren't baptized as infants? What would I do if they decided to follow Islam like their father? What if they fell in with the wrong crowd? Sure, there were good immigrant communities in the area, but there were dangerous people too. She gets more fervent as she goes on, but finally, after what feels far too long, she begins to wind down. I let her talk, wary of saying something that sparks her energy again.

I don't want to fight. I know I have no hope against Susan's sharp tongue in an argument, not when I'm feeling fragile with this rolling, tossing stomach. I end up thanking her for thinking about be, but I know what I'm doing and am an adult who can make my own decisions. She stops a sound in her throat, and I can tell she's stopping herself from starting a new discussion. She's barely holding back from critiquing my response, calling it flippant or dismissive. Instead, she nods.

I am shaken as I leave. Even though Susan gives me a hug after we step out, my arms are clammy and dead against her back. My goodbye is dull and doesn't mean anything. I wonder if Susan can tell how insincere I'm feeling now. I thanked her. Why did I do that? It was meant to shut down the conversation, but it still left a sour feeling in my mouth, like I had somehow validated the need for her concern.

As I walk, I pay attention to the people around me on the street. I'd always loved the diversity of my city and was shaken that someone else didn't see it in the same way that I did: as something special. Jamal was a magnifying glass in my life; while the sun illuminated and shone down on all that I love, Jamal was the focal point that intensified and concentrated my attention. He helped identify my passions and narrow my many interests down to the few that I could focus on and follow with more dedication. It was because of his support and encouragement that my first anthology chapter was getting published. It was because of him that I expanded my horizons, ate at Precious Restaurant, finally got around to having dinner at The Taste of Ghana. Jamal didn't limit me; he broadened my horizons.

It's several weeks before I pass by Costa on a walk. I take a step towards it out of habit, but my stomach tightens in a knot the moment I veer to the door. Memories of the conversation with Susan flood my mind, and all I can feel is the confusing boiled blend of anger, the desire to flee. My foot finds it pace as I continue forward.

I go to a lot of smaller coffee shops, the independent ones, like my mother always wanted. I find out they are just as wonderful, each with their own vibe and specialties. I move beyond hot chocolate and get more adventurous in what I drink. Turns out I really like lattes.

Over summer I get involved with teaching adult education classes. I teach reading and writing to people from all over. I meet Leela, and we become fast friends. I start to visit her family on the occasional weekend. I cherish the new experiences and culture I get to experience in the same city where I grew up.

I go to a mosque. At first, I'm intimidated by the green dome on top, the angled windows and how it looks almost like a school; the differences make the familiarity seem strange. The gates are beautiful though, crescent moons and stars welcoming me in, the tops of the fence a gilded golden colour. The people at the Islamic Centre are friendly and welcoming, and I am more assured that this is a community with which I feel comfortable growing closer.

When I walk around or run errands with my mother during my visits, I pay attention to the places I know. I reflect. I realize they're not defined by any single encounter. The grocery store wasn't just the place where I turned my ankle, it's also where I got the ingredients to make my first blancmange. It's where I went to resupply the pantry every week after I learned how much I loved rhubarb. Bede Park wasn't defined by my screaming match with Jane, it was also where I watched my cousin play, wild, rampant, and utterly filled with glee on the playground. Each place is defined by more than one encounter, more than one person.

Jamal and I get married. The wedding is beautiful, and we have readings from the Koran, the Bible, and Wordsworth. I barely notice Susan at the wedding. I'm too focused on the love.

I carry that love with me as I go through my days. I work to find the love for each place I visit by searching through my memories. The more I do this, the easier it becomes to remember the importance of each site. The good memories overshadow the bad until all I can think of for each place is a collage of smiles, laughter, and new discoveries.

It is three years before I go to Costa again. This time when I go, I know what I want to order.

This time, the teacake tastes sweet.

CAROL LEEMING MBE, FRSA.
CURVE LEICESTER - A GLORIOUS UNDULATING THOUGHT

Poem performed to a special audience of 1,447 live by Carol Leeming to celebrate Curve Live! Curve Theatre 10th Birthday Celebrations 2018. Kind thanks to Nikolai Foster Artistic Director and Chris Stafford CEO.

Curve is a vaulted band
Constructed from big imaginations
With tessellated windows of light
-a steel glass compound eye
It frames all its surroundings

Curve is a musical chamber
Composed by capricious winds
With vibrating walls of voices
-a brick plaster speaker box
It sings all of its own songs

Curve is an artistic taste
Created by artists with diligent levity
With heart stopping eye-watering acts
-a black box sublime canvas
It frees all audiences to escape

Curve is a thrilling encounter
Forged chances of dreamed visions
With busied offices of keen activity
-a desk computer open hive
It makes all dreams come true

Curve is a marvelous fabrication
Manufactured artifices by deft artisans
With ingenious studio workshops
-a driven factory of fantasy
It creates all things awe inspiring

Curve is a street art rainbow
Spotted coloured beams show the way

With gleaming light for us to shine
-a crystal prism for us to enter
It opens all its doors to a world of stars

Curve is a bowl it holds up our dreams
For them to float far above high on its roof
Fortified ground secures as it cushions Curve
If you listen closely it throbs with echoes
Of pounding music, the sweat of wild
Reveries past of the Long Ship, Rondezvous
Clubs, LUCA Dances distant as radio waves

This chosen ground only tolerated joyful
Congregations those tirelessly in pursuit
Of magic, luminosity, oneness,
Togetherness, kindled by the love of
The universal human spirit embraced here
Still, it blazes like a fire I once saw lit on Curve's Stage
Long may Curve continue to swell bend undulate
Liberate us always, to make big waves of change.

SARAH KIRBY
THE TURKEY CAFÉ

JULIE GARDNER
LOUGHBOROUGH FAIR

Last on the bus before it leaves the town,
he shuffles to his seat, greets
 a woman known to him, "Hey Linda,
have you been on them rides again?"
She laughs, "You wouldn't want to see that Bert."

They talk about the fair, how it's changed
since they were kids,
how high and fast and loud it is.

He gets off the bus in front of me.
Limps home alone.

AWUAH MAINOO GABRIEL

Hails from Accra and is a poet, lyricist and a Playwright, studying at the
University of Cape Coast. His work, 'Taunt', won best satire of 2016 on Voices
of African Poets. His first published work 'Afri-lad', appeared on the Africa
Alliance of YMCAs website. He has featured in many magazines.

PARADISE FOUND

Here is another home to call home
When we are away from home
Once a wife's nag becomes too pleasant for a song
We present ourselves for a wholly reconnection
Within the divine landscape of Hollycroft
And as we go with clouded hearts
And deep wrinkles of strife and office weariness
We fasten ourselves to better moments
And wring out the boredom off our sodden sleeves.

Though nature was meant for healing
But first the home of the spirit must be healthy
If it is sports that must heal us
So go on, hold on to rackets
And as we swing from base to base
We begin living the essence of love through reciprocality
If it is putting that must free us
So we go on
To putt the troubles zillion miles away the feet of Leicester
And if it is bowling that must bring delight
So go on Jack
Roll roll, roll the rolling ball.

And to the desires of the spirit
O, sing to us blessed Hollycroft
You mighty trees
You murmuring wind
You choral birds
Give us the chords.

Speak to us you ambience of paradise
Tell us
How the hanging fire sneaks into these boughs
To mount serene pavilions upon us
What beauty
What peace
What elegance
O, what home I find beneath the skin of Hinckley!

HANNAH ESPLIN

Is 16 years old. She currently lives in a very small town called Dereham.
Writing poetry is a rather new thing for her and she hopes to further develop
her skills in the future. Hannah is currently taking an A-Level in English
Language and Literature.

LEICESTER

Away from my home,
My mother tongue forces me
To yearn for my love
My Leicester.

Like a moth to a flame
I flock to River Soar
Envelope myself in that familiar water.
Baptise myself within it.

Now blessed by my Holy land,
I clutch my memories in hand
As close to my heart
As a lost love.

The forever savoured memories
Of this long forgotten feeling,
Walking on wrong pavements
And reminiscing about those right ones

The Earth beneath my feet,
Here,
Only here,
Does it feel so accepting.

Those often disregarded trees
Wave back to me
As I run down those streets,
A child once again

The wind in my hair
How does it feel different here?
The scent of nostalgia
Fills my lungs

An antique person is born today.
I see my reflection in the river
I am no longer who I am,
But the young 7 year old me.

Smile bright as the sun,
Eyes wider than wide,
My scrunched up little nose,
And my deepest dimples.

I am where I am meant to be.
In Leicester,
The place of memories.
This place of mine.

PHIL HOWARD

Is a local authority worker who would like to see poetry restored as an art form which can be appreciated by all through relevant and accessible work that tackles compelling subject matter. Some of his newer poetry has been published in various anthologies and on websites.

THE KING SPEAKS IN LEICESTER

I was the King of England, certainly,
so on that day when my fate was sealed,
when at last I fell on the battlefield,
it was only right and proper that they bore me,
my broken and brutalised body,
my mortal remains, to Greyfriars where monks kneeled
in prayer as the monastery bells pealed,
broadcasting Henry Tudor's victory.
I suppose that it was the will of God
that I should lose my crown, the strangest of things;
from God I drew my legitimacy,
my right to rule, so why should it have been me
that perished at Bosworth Field? It seems odd.
And what price now the Divine Right of Kings?

HUI-LING CHEN

Is from Taiwan. She is a PhD researcher at De Montfort University, her
research is about Adult Education & Art Education. She had poems published
in the anthologies "Welcome to Leicester", "Leicester 2084 AD: New Poems
about The City", and "Small Acts of Kindness."

LEICESTER INTO THE BLUE

Leicester City Blue blends into sky.

When people look up,
their imagination expands,
up through the atmosphere into eternity,
the unpredictable future.

Their minds fly with the whole city when colours merge.
There's a reason for Leicester Blue:
the limitless possibilities.

EMMA LEE

Emma Lee's recent collection is "Ghosts in the Desert" (IDP, UK 2015). "The Significance of a Dress" is forthcoming from Arachne. She co-edited "Over Land, Over Sea," (Five Leaves, UK, 2015), reviews for The Blue Nib, High Window Journal, The Journal, London Grip, Sabotage Reviews and her blog at emmalee1.wordpress.com.

LITTER PICK AT SCRAPTOFT HALL

The ladies of eighteen-sixty-one no doubt picked up
after themselves at their fund-raising afternoon tea,
one shilling buying a china cup and tea cake.

Today I'm picking up single-use coffee cups
shadowed by the hall that still has eighteenth century
Lady Leticia Wigley's initials in its facade.

Her lake's grey sorrow more fitting
to the First World War and Scraptoft's only fallen
solider remembered in Corah Close.

I'd have been collecting confetti during the second.
Herb, a parachutist, then camped on the golf course
fell for Iris. Now in their nineties and still together.

During the college years, I'd imagine my haul
would be sweet and other wrappers, a post-exam
bonfire of notes and tickets to the comedy festival.

Today's pick of fast food wrappers and losing
lottery tickets, a spare two pence, merely a collection
of ordinary stories barely worth recording.

LAURA LEWIS-WATERS
A keen traveller and environmental enthusiast from the Midlands, Laura has lived on three continents and has a little something published in all three. Having studied Literature, History, Creative Writing and Volcanology, she is now currently teaching at secondary school and doing occasional research for a PhD.

WELCOME TO LEICESTERSHIRE

At the low bridge on the border
Where the ghosts of old bears rise
To face those of aged kings
Chains clanking like Marley
I am beckoned across the seams by
Welcome to Leicestershire
Where I am content on coiling roads lined with treetop gold
Beside the River Mease.

Greeted by postcard villages Nailstone, Barlestone, Congerstone
Originally from Atherstone
The charming acquaintances give way to the National Forest –
A National Treasure
A heart in the Midlands, heart of the country.

When the soft autumnal blanket begins to lift at the edges
And I see the familiar brown sign of the Battlefield Line
We make a final pilgrimage to Bradgate Park
The verdant green visible across distant borders
Confirmed by the map: *Sliding Stone Enclosure, Deer Park Spinney, Coppice Plantation*
And deer agree to roam free
The true *heart of rural England*
Thank you for driving carefully.

KATARZYNA J SZOPKA

Is a writer from Poland. She is a student at University of Leicester with a degree in Criminology. She's always been full of ideas. When she started education, she participated in many poetry competitions, and even won a few. Wolves and other wild animals fascinate her.

RATAE CORIELTAUVORUM
(LEICESTER)

The light dances on a cobalt pathway,
Like a young Roman girl who lived here back then...
The moon shines on an onyx sky,
Like Roman soldiers gallea.
Grey stones sprinkled with sapphire blood,
Blood of queens and kings,
Who were not given chance to see the end of summer.
We who walk the same boulevards as they did
We are engraved in stones around us.
The golden locks of time...
Tangle us together.
Allow us to live together,
Till the end of days.

MUIR SPERRINGS

Discovered writing ten years ago when writing a Eulogy for her aunt. Since then Muir's been on writing courses, taking inspiration from the surrounding countryside and the city. Opposite her flat on the edge of Leicester City, is a plot left to badgers, foxes and various insects, a veritable stimulus.

GALLOWTREE GATE

The sun gives out a golden glow
as upon a marbled seat I muse
and then, from an open cafe door
a catchy thrum of distant strings.

My eyes open, as I look around
at people dancing as they pass.
There's elegance in shocking pink
and roughness in an old grey hat.

Earrings glitter as a head is tossed
loose jowls sink into shirt of silk
when suddenly my vision fractures
as feet on skateboards rumble past.

Time silently and swiftly moves
as town hall clock strikes eleven
I gather up all my shopping
and hurry along the avenue.

Pushing open the frosted doors
three minutes late; my friends are there
at our favourite meeting place
relaxed in comfy leather chairs.

The hourglass falls, our coffees drunk,
We say our heartfelt goodbyes
and step out into the busy street
to head for home by bus and car.

SARAH KIRBY
LEICESTER CATHEDRAL

MAGGIE SCOTT MBE

72, a mother and grandmother, writes poetry, short stories and children's fiction for her own enjoyment. Born in Sheffield and raised in Barnsley, she moved to Leicester in 1968 to start teaching. In 2018 she retired after 50 years at Forest Lodge Primary School. She's received three lifetime achievement awards.

DANIEL LAMBERT

In 1770, on a sunny March morn
In Leicester, Daniel Lambert was born.
He soon began to weigh a lot
And the more he grew, the wider he got.
By the time he was twenty three years old,
He was thirty two stone, or so we are told.

Bred of country stock, healthy and fit,
He reared dogs and cocks and rode horses a bit.
An animal breeder of some renown,
He once fought a bear in Leicester town.
He'd loved his sport and was very strong,
But in 1805 things were to go wrong.

Now, the heaviest man in history,
(How he kept going remains a mystery),
He lost his job in charge of the Jail,
And all his assets were doomed to fail.
So, at thirty six, he became quite willing
To exhibit himself, for the price of a shilling.

He toured the country, enjoying the fame,
Charging people to see his frame.
In Stamford he stayed at a well-known Inn.
There, as he was washing and shaving his chin,
He put his cut throat razor aside,
And suddenly, collapsed and died.

They couldn't remove his body at all
And in the end they knocked down a wall.
He weighed fifty-two stone and eleven pound
And his girth was nine foot four all around.
Twenty men lowered his coffin down
Into his grave in Stamford town.

At Newarke Houses, in Leicester, today
His clothes and belongings are on display
And although Daniel Lambert has long since gone
He remains Leicester's hero and favourite son.

JULIA WOOD
*Holds a Masters' Degree in Continental Philosophy from Warwick University
and has published The Resurrection of Oscar Wilde: A Cultural Afterlife. Her
Victorian clothes and house style receive media exposure and she enjoys the
publicity process as much as the writing.*

DAY PASS TO LEICESTER

Oscar Wilde stood nervously at the gateway to the world he had left behind in
1900. A slight-built man appeared at his side.

"Pav. Your tour guide for the day."

He looked Oscar up and down, doubtless taking in Oscar's dark velvet suit, the
waved shoulder length hair. "I wonder what they will make of you in
Leicester."

"Pav - it is pleasure to meet you."

Oscar clutched the white lily he always carried - because, he had discovered,
religion may fail but flowers never let one down. Oscar shook Pav's hand,
surmising this slender creature was not much more than a boy.

"Oscar."

"I know who you are, it is great honour, my friend."

Pav smiled, showing white, even teeth.

"Do not be nervous. We go on special day - a day you like."

Oscar nodded, mystified by this comment. They were travelling to
Leicester Earth by Astro-train, a portal that facilitated movement between
planes of existence, and down which, Oscar discovered, one always travelled
backwards.

"This is like watching video of Doctor Who on rewind, no?"

Oscar hadn't the faintest idea what Pav was talking about, but his accent
delighted him.

"Ah, you speak like a character from Bram Stoker's Dracula," he
exclaimed.

Pav laughed.

"You very educated man. You compare everything to art?"

"My dear - life, such as it is, can only be viewed through the lens of art -
it is the only means through which it exists."

"Here we are," Pav interjected. "Welcome to Leicester."

172

Oscar looked around with a sense of wonder, at the old brick structure of the building; doubtless built in his time. Within that structure were glass doors, rows of black beetle-like things that he recognised as cabs. The place was noisy and smelt poisonous. People scurried about, a voice, artificially loud and full of echo, made Oscar jump - "the next train to arrive at Platform Two is the eleven fifteen to Birmingham New Street, calling at…"

Everywhere was loud and overwhelming. Without warning his heart began racing. He closed his eyes. He was handcuffed in the pouring rain wearing the absurd stripes of the prison garb; people laughed and jeered, his name was screeched from coarse lips like a profanity - Oscar Wilde! A man moved towards him; spit landed on his cheek.

"You okay, my friend?"

Oscar opened his eyes and let out a sigh. He could feel his body shaking; his legs felt weak.

"Railway stations…alas, they do not hold sweet memories for me, but bitter ones." Oscar explained to Pav how, six months after his arrest he had stood at Clapham Junction during his transfer from Wandsworth to Reading Gaol on that icy November of 1895, surrounded by a jeering mob.

Pav turned pale. "My grandparents - they ran away from Poland, to escape the Nazis. But many more - friends, cousins, neighbours - they were not so lucky." Pav swallowed hard. "See, like you I have darkness in my past." Oscar gave him a reassuring smile. He had heard of the Nazis. Its horror had filtered through to the afterlife, told in the stories of those who had passed.

"I am sad for you," he said.

"You not worry now. I lived in Leicester. You are safe here. We are both safe here. This is twenty-first century."

Right now, more than anything Oscar wanted to catch the next Astro-train back to the afterlife. It was a long time since he had been offered a day pass. The last time had been in the nineteen-twenties, and he had declined, saying he was busy with a séance that day. In truth he had not been ready. The memory of the public opprobrium that had settled around him had still been too raw and painful.

Pav, obviously sensing Oscar's reticence, said, "It good you have day pass. Don't waste it. It usually Elvis who get day out on Earth. He waste it, he go to launderette and sing, 'Nothing but Hound Dog.'"

Oscar smiled. He had yet to meet this Elvis character, but they moved, it seemed, in different social circles.

"You hungry?"

Oscar nodded. It was a strange and unfamiliar feeling, the emptiness in his belly. Spirit did not eat. They lived on the compliments that came through during séances.

"You like curry?"

The weather, he noticed after he had passed out of the station, was bright and warm; people were in short sleeves and short trousers; there were women in trousers, which was not so unusual - his friend, the great Sarah Bernhardt had worn trousers - but the biggest surprise of all was the women in short skirts and top garments so flimsy they reminded him of the Victorian camisoles.

He walked past a brick building with the sign Blunts above it. It was crammed with shoes and boots that did not seem to differ greatly from the ones worn in his day. He saw that they sold shoes by Clarks too. In the midst of all the noise and unfamiliarity this oasis of continuity brought him a strange comfort. He noted the name of the street - Granby Street.

He looked to Pav, silently at his side. He addressed him in a soft voice. "You are very young. How did you pass?" That was always the question in the afterlife - not do you come here often? - but how did you die?

"Ah, that is a story. I deliver food; I was working for Deliveroo," he replied, as they passed a shop called Life Charity Shop.

"Deliveroo?" Oscar raised a quizzical eyebrow.

"They are food company, see? They deliver food to…person's house. I work for them when I was on Earth. And one day I cycle up London Road with food, and - motor scooter - it knock me into road and bang! I get run over by number thirty-one bus. It go to Oadby. I go to…paradise."

"Oh dear, I am indeed sad for you." Oscar paused thoughtfully. "You are an immigrant - as was I. I am sorry that England did not treat you better."

"She treated you far worse, my Irish friend. I read your life and I weep."

"Do not be in sorrow for me," Oscar said.

Pav smiled.

"Now, we go to Clock Tower and get bus."

On the opposite side of the road they passed a red and white building that said HSBC. Oscar stared in fascination at the little cubby holes lined up outside. People were standing at them, their backs to the passers by. He was about to ask Pav why they had confession boxes in the street, when Pav touched his arm.

"We are now at Clock Tower. See this building…?"

Pav indicated a tall thin brick structure with a clock on it.

"It is just like Magdalen Tower, in my beloved Oxford," Oscar replied, enthralled.

At the Clock Tower a man was shouting,

"Jesus said, 'I am the resurrection and the life.'"

Oscar smiled.

"Today, I am the Resurrection." He pondered this.

"I wonder if my tomb is empty."

"No, your tomb, it crowded with tourists and fans of the Smiths."

Oscar shook his head in bewilderment. He watched in wonder as crowds of people waving flags with rainbows painted on them swarmed along, singing and cheering. He stared interestedly at the logo on the flags. "LGBTQI," he read.

Pav smiled.

"See. You like. It stands for 'Lesbian Gay Bisexual Transgender Questioning Intersex.'"

"That is a lot of people asking questions about sex. And they have not been arrested?"

"No, my friend. Intersex, means people who are…what you would call…between genders."

"Between genders," Oscar repeated, intrigued. "Like the Hermaphrodites, how incredible that the myths of old now walk the earth."

"If you say so, my friend." Pav smiled.

"What a truly colourful place Leicester is." Oscar smiled as another couple in sparkling silver walked past, wrapped in a rainbow flag. "There were never any rainbows in London. Only fogs."

Fifteen minutes later they disembarked onto a street that thronged with women in glittering garments which, Oscar noted, draped from the shoulders in a Grecian style. Never an advocate of the corset he considered these women to be the walking ideals of Dress Reform, the drapes pleasingly following the natural shape of the body.

The shop windows displayed brightly coloured garments and the air smelled of fine, exotic spices.

"Welcome to the Golden Mile, my friend."

"The Golden Mile! How charming this is. It is like India but with clouds."

"You have been to India?"

Oscar shook his head.

"I speak with the wisdom of inexperience."

"You are funny, my velvet friend."

"I am never more serious than when I am funny."

Pav laughed.

"I thought here."

He stopped outside a restaurant that had Bobby's written above it.

"It is vegetarian."

"Oh, do vegetarians eat then?"

Pav laughed.

"Of course."

Oscar, forgetting himself, made to walk through the door, feeling its solidity colliding with that of his body. Stunned, he stepped back.

"Ah, you think you are still particles, no?"

Pav pushed open the door and held it for Oscar, who was more bruised in pride than body. Oscar hoped no one had seen that. He had been a dandy, a man of fashion. Walking into doors was not how he cared to be remembered.

They entered into a large, glass fronted space. The smell of spices was stronger than the one outside, mingled with a burning smell.

A thin looking man in a red apron approached them. "Can I help you?"

"Yes, table for two please?" Pav said.

After they had been seated and were studying the menus Oscar became aware of a couple, reading from the menu and of one girl, a red head, who exclaimed, "Paneer tikk-oh masal-oh," excitedly.

Oscar wondered what tikk-oh masah-loh was. After finding only paneer tikka masala on the menu, which admittedly sounded tasty, he puzzled over the question while Pav engaged himself with reading the menu.

The waiter was standing at their side. "Can I take your order?"

Pav glanced at Oscar, who nodded.

"One vegetable tandoori and garlic naan," Pav said.

"What is paneer tikk-oh, masa-loh?" Oscar said.

"You want paneer tikka masala?" the waiter said.

Pav erupted into laughter. "He not from round here, see."

Bemused, Oscar ordered the dish and pilau rice to go with it, at the recommendation of the waiter.

After the waiter had taken their order and left, Pav took it upon himself to explain to Oscar the peculiar inflections of the Leicester accent, all of which Oscar found highly amusing.

"So, you do not say Oadby, you say Oad-beh. And hello is, it is ay up me duck?"

"That's it. It funny for me too, when I first came here."

"How curious. I see shall have to learn this interesting new dialect if I am to communicate with the people of Leicester, I mean, Lest-ah."

Oscar noticed the redhead staring at him.

"Don't I know you from somewhere?" she said.

"I think not, my dear, though it is pleasant to make your acquaintance."

"I do! I know you, from the telly. Are you filming here?"

Oscar knew what a telly was. He had met David Bowie just after Bowie had passed and they had formed a great friendship based on a passion for reinvention.

"Mr Ross!"

She said. For a moment Oscar thought she must be referring to his dear friend, Robbie Ross, whom he had known during his time on Earth and who had been at his deathbed.

Now, a few other people in the restaurant were looking and the murmur of voices began, "It's Jonathan Ross, what's he doing here?"

"Ay up me duck! Will you sign my serviette?"

A man who looked in his thirties stood in front of Oscar, holding out a crumpled white thing.

"I don't have any paper," he explained.

Oscar paused, looking to Pav. Who on earth was Jonathan Ross?

"My dear man, I think you are mistaken."

Oscar turned away. The man stepped in front of him.

"It's for my wife. She has such a crush on you; it's that floppy hair thing you got going on."

On an impulse, Oscar decided to humour him. After all, where was the harm?

The man passed him a thin stick-like thing. Oscar examined it closely.

"You have an inkwell?"

"It's a biro. You don't need ink, see?" Pav said to Oscar in a low voice. Oscar took up the pen and to his surprise as he pressed it to the serviette the words Jonathan Ross formed in his thin looped writing. It was quite magical, a pen that produced its own ink, a sort of bejewelled glass squid.

"Thanks, my wife will be chuffed to little mint balls."

"What a curious turn of phrase you have," Oscar said.

The man moved in closer.

"You sure you're Jonathan Ross? You don't talk like him."

Oscar struggled to fight the familiar panic.

"Oh well, nice to meet you anyway," the man said.

After the man had returned to his seat Oscar and Pav chatted quietly, though Oscar was aware of the occasional stares and mutterings.

A woman in a carnation-green silk coat glanced at him and said,

"I'm sure that's Stephen Fry."

Oscar caught his breath.

"Nah," her male companion replied.

"It's that chat show guy, what's his name…"

Oscar let out a deep sigh.

"Who is Stephen Fry?" he said quietly.

"He play you, in film of your life, he actor, see?"

"I hope he played me better than I did. My final scenes are in great need of improvement."

"I have not seen film, but I doubt that very much."

Oscar realised he must still look anxious, as Pav said,

"It is okay, my friend. This is not your Victorian England. Trust me. I will show you."

After they had eaten and left the restaurant Oscar became aware of a burning in his mouth.

"You okay?"

Oscar nodded.

"That food was…" he huffed out a breath

"…quite spiced, like the fire of Arabia. It has turned my tongue into a flame, my throat into a road of tiny fires."

Pav laughed.

"You are still the poet."

Together they caught another bus back to the centre of Leicester and when there Oscar saw more crowds; banners and colourfully dressed people. Men in tutus and wigs, people with flags bearing rainbows wrapped around themselves, faces striped with rainbows.

"You know, Leicester is quite the thing. I think…when my time comes to leave the other world, I shall come and live here, in this land of spices and rainbows."

"It is not always like this, but today, today is Pride so we celebrate."

"Pride?"

"We go now, to Pride on the park."

Oscar thrilled at the atmosphere, the crowds and the colour as he let his friend lead the way, out of the centre and back up what he now recognised as London Road.

As they reached the edge of the park which, it transpired, was called Victoria Park, the music became almost unbearably loud. It was an unfamiliar sound, lots of percussion, and people dancing. There was a gate area where it seemed people were being checked in by men dressed in black uniforms. Oscar stepped back and sucked in his breath.

"You all right, my friend?"

Oscar took a moment to compose himself.

"They are Security."

He let out a sigh of relief. It was peculiar how the body remembered trauma even when the mind did not.

He walked with Pav and they had their hands stamped with a symbol that reminded Oscar of a postal stamp. It felt strange to be of the flesh again, the very solidity of his body amazed him. He had been pure light for so long, that to be of earthly things again gave him a sense of heaviness that was hard to get used to. He took in the scenes, the men kissing, the people dressed up, walking with banners, laughing, hugging.

Pav explained to him the reason for this, it was a yearly celebration of Pride.

"In my day we called it Uranian love," Oscar said. "But in my day the love that dared not speak its name had yet to clear its throat."

Pav smiled.

Oscar fought the sadness that threatened to fill him; the sadness that came from wanting to be in this new, accepting world; the sorrow that he and his darling Bosie had not lived their lives in a better world. He thought of his final days on Earth; the small hotel room around which the increasingly narrow circumference of his life evolved, the dwindling friends, the extinction of the creative impulse, by the end, quite gone out, like a candle at one of Madam Blavatsky's séances. He shook these memories away.

"My dear boy," Oscar said. "I had thought paradise was in the other world. I had no idea it had come to this one."

Slowly, a crowd was moving towards Oscar. This time he felt strangely relaxed; intoxicated by the Dionysian atmosphere of celebration and revelry.

"Stephen! Stephen!"

They were shouting. A few were holding up their little oblong objects and clicking. Pav smiled.

"Just play along with them."

Oscar rolled his eyes good-naturedly.

A man in tight leather shorts and a tiny top approached him, took his hand and kissed it.

"You were brill-yant in Wilde! It's a modern love storeh, you and Bonsai."

"Bosie," Oscar corrected, smiling. "Though he was just as exotic a flower and quite as difficult to nurture."

"I think It's dead good you've come to Lest-oh for Pride. Anyway,'ow a ya?"

Oscar was glad of the emergency Leicester lessons he had from Pav in the restaurant.

"I am very well thank-you, and yourself?"

"Yeah, I'm good, mate. I'm Mick by the way. Can I ave me picture taken wi' yoh?"

"Er…of course."

Seeing Pav, Mick handed the camera and Oscar politely posed with Mick, while Pav clicked away. Pav handed the camera back to Mick.

"Nice to meet ya, take care of yourself, duck," Mick said.

With that he walked away with a little wave and a wiggle of his rather fetching behind.

"It okay," Pav said. "You ghost. You not come out on photo."

Oscar felt a touch disappointed - and after he had posed so artfully too.

Now, a queue began to form, of people holding out pieces of paper. More people clicked away on their cameras. All had pens at the ready, and Oscar dutifully wrote Stephen Fry on each of their pieces of paper. He had in his last years, been Sebastian Melmoth, to spare the blushes of the postman so adopting alternate identities was something he had become used to.

After the queue had abated Oscar said to Pav,

"It really is quite extraordinary how many people look like me these days. The thing is becoming a perfect delight."

Across the park Oscar noticed a woman, most curiously attired. She seemed dressed as the people of his time, only with garments a touch lighter. She was in faded florals, with a pink hat bedecked with flowers. Dark ringlets tumbled past her shoulders. He watched her scanning the area, as he signed the autographs.

Now, a man in female attire was approaching him. He was, Oscar would say, of foreign persuasion, Indian maybe. He wore a long white dress and had thick black hair falling about his shoulders.

"Come and dance!"

He grabbed Oscar by the hand and led him towards the stage, where the music played, it seemed to pour from tall black oblong boxes, though there was no one on the stage. The rhythm of the music was exotic, like nothing he had heard. Oscar, for all his flamboyance, had never been a dancer, but now he let the moment take him. He twirled around with this striking looking man and Pav came to join them, and together they twirled and danced.

"You've got to love Kylie!" the man said.

"Love the clothes, by the way. They're so Oscar Wilde. Are you a fan?"

"He huge fan," Pav said, winking at Oscar, who laughed.

It was, Oscar conceded, easy to move to this music, and so he swayed gently, letting his hair fall over his face, feeling the sweat on his brow as men in pairs, and women in pairs walked past holding hands. Each time a couple walked by Oscar became aware of little more of the heaviness of the past falling away. After the music had finished the Indian man smiled,

"Great to meet you."

He drifted off towards a white tent near the entrance.

Oscar spied the women in the hat again. She stood at a distance, now singing along to the music. After the crowded had dispersed he turned his attention to this curiously attired woman.

"Who is that?" he asked Pav.

Pav looked to where Oscar pointed.

"I don't know her name. She... like to dress in the old fashions."

"Is she a ghost?"

Pav shook his head.

"She know words to Kylie Minogue, so she not ghost, no. She lives here. In Leicester."

Now she was staring at him and Oscar made to approach her, but Pav put a hand on his arm.

"It is time to go my friend. We must not miss the Astro-train."

"Ah, to miss any more Astro-trains would expose us to comment on the platform."

Pav smiled.

Oscar met the lady's gaze. She walked up to him, looked again and Oscar thought he saw tears in her eyes. He noticed she had one hand cupped over her belly. Something passed between them, something indefinable. He did not know her but he would come to know her, and soon because it was almost time. That much he understood. Then, she said in a whisper,

"Oscar."

She wiped a stray tear. Oscar was about to ask her name when he began to feel the solidity and the earthiness of his form waning. He moved away. He must not alarm the lady by turning into particles in front of her. It would be an act of indecent explosion.

Before the lady could say more, he and Pav had floated away, back towards the station, to the Astro-train that would take them back to the dimension from whence they had come.

And now Oscar felt lighter - the pain of the past had at last removed its leaden weight. He had become whole again, mended. He was ready.

"One more thing before we go," Pav said. "Trip Advisor."

Back in the familiar lightness of his own dimension Oscar wondered what those who searched Trip Advisor would make of his review.

He had, of course, awarded it five stars and written, 'When bad people die, they go to paradise. When good people die, they go to Leicester.' He had signed it, Oscar Wilde, with a 'P.S. I will be back.'

"No one will believe it was you, my friend," Pav said.

"Ah, I am like God. I am quite used to people who do not believe in me."

EMMA LEE

A WINDOW IN THE ANGEL GATEWAY

If you can judge a civilisation by how well it looks after its vulnerable citizens,
can you judge a city by how well it looks after its alleyways?
Are they ill-kempt receptacles for refuse or graffiti-free and maintained?

The Angel Gateway follows a former right of way
through what was the Angel Inn's yourd. A momentary shelter
from the lively market and bustle of Gallowtree Gate.

Mary Queen of Scots spent two nights here en route
to Fotheringhaye before her execution. Did she find
a dash of colour in the grey, a temporary window of hope?

There's a window here now, tucked above a drainpipe and behind
iron bars with lattice work, stained blue squares drawing attention
to a central diamond like an imprisoned eye trying to look up and out.

IONA MANDAL
EVER THE SAME

Here Diwali lights down Belgrave Road
shine onto the neighbourhood church.
Here tolerance reigns supreme.
Hence, Gary Lineker hails a Mahatma Gandhi statue
as masala curries and pies unite people.
Here history entwines with the National Space Centre
unearthed from cark parks, sleeping kings arise,
a sari could have been his burial shroud.
No one is a minority here
instead, each proud to be ethnically diverse.
My place, my identity, my social glue
Semper Eadem
Leicester.

STEPHEN WYLIE

*Was born in Glasgow a long time ago, but his early life was spent mostly in
Ayrshire. Upon graduating from Glasgow University, he moved to Leicester,
and has been here ever since. He took up writing late in life and has had poetry
published in three local anthologies.*

SWANS IN THE NIGHT

On Mile Straight the swans are sleeping;
only one a watch is keeping.
The others float on current free,
heads laid upon their backs.
Lost in dream,
they let the stream
take them where it will.

MAGGIE SCOTT MBE
THE BATTLE OF BOSWORTH

When Edward IV died, his two young heirs
Were denied the crown, which was rightly theirs.
The Duke of York took over all power
And locked the princes in The Tower.
Richard, the Duke, began to reign
And the boys were never seen again.
But Henry Tudor, exiled in France,
Sought to be king and took his chance.
He came to fight with his Lancastrian knights
And claim the crown which was his by rights.
To a field at Bosworth two armies arrived.
They fought to the death, but Henry survived
And as Richard fell on that blood-stained field,
The Yorkist army was forced to yield.
The crown of England rolled on the ground
Under a bush, where it was found
By a Lancastrian soldier, who held it up high,
To the roar of the victors gathered close by.
Henry was crowned in a field full of clover
And the Wars of the Roses were finally over.
York's body was placed on his horse
And taken to Leicester, where, in due course,
He was buried at Greyfriars and there lies a mystery,
That is now a part of Leicester's history.
It seems Richard's body was left to rot
Under a car park (and x marked the spot!)

AMY WEBB

Is a 15 year old student from Birmingham. She is an avid public speaker and an aspiring poet. She writes and speaks about mental health in hopes of raising awareness and to hopefully give hope to those who are suffering and inspire them that recovery is possible. She also talks about other issues found in modern society.

IN THE HEART OF OUR CITIES

In the heart of our cities
Surrounded by a world of hate
Because we cannot mate
Battling colours of skins
And the sexualities within
We may never win
But we shall not sin
Amongst broken parts
Where do we start
On broken streets
In broken cities
In the heart of our cities
Towns filled with frowns
Worn like crowns.

In the heart of our cities
Rounded knives
Fight within
Amongst silver blades
Lay empty sleeping bags
Amongst the empty corpses
A city full of lost hope
Painted in colour
But grey
They may prey
But we are lost.

In the heart of our cities
Grey lights may shine
Buildings in line
In the heart of our cities,
Women breathless against cold floor
Hands tied against bed posts
Men abuse the law
But behind closed doors.

In the heart of our cities
Teenagers hang from ropes
Smoking dope
Street corners loitered
The future.

In the heart of our cities
Black and bruised
Broken and wounded
Forced down and pounded
But still
In a GCSE hall
Standing tall
But she was abused too
In the heart of our cities
Open our eyes
Believe we are the future
We nurture
We mature

In the heart of our cities,
Angry words darted across,
Sirens echo,
Death has found him a throne,
Far down within the west,
But we have seen the worst and the best.

In the heart of our cities.
Abandoned children
Mothers school clothed
Single mothers who want a life
For their children amongst the rife
In our city
In every city
There is beauty
Amongst the pity
In our city
We are born in this city
Leicester is where we were born
We own it,
We have no shame.
In the heart of the cities,
In Leicester,
There is no shame.

ERIN P. DOOLEY

Is an artist and scientist from NYC/Wales who has recently moved to Leicestershire. She likes to take photos and to write and has found much inspiration in the surrounding countryside.

OLD OWSTON ROAD

Waxed Barbour cracked at elbows
and seams
Like furrows and streams
near Old Owston Road

Autumn rambles stark muddy fields
land stripped of yields
near Old Owston Road

LISA WILLIAMS
LEWIS'S 1979

The whole store really was a relic to times past, even back then. The old
escalator hid in the middle by the sized glove display.
Its black looping rubber handrail ran over sides of polished oak. Sturdy art deco
curves buffed to a high shine from years of waxing. The symmetry made it like
an instrument, a mammoth cello or maybe a double bass.
It shook as we stood, just as my Mum had with her Mum all those years before,
tentative on rickety wooden slats. It screeched as it climbed, struggling on its
weary way up to Santa's grotto.

PAM THOMPSON
BLACK SPIDERS

September, 1945, a plague of black spiders. Some said it was unseasonal heat
that brought them away from the cities and onto the land. Others said that they
were an omen, or a charm, like the green acorns with snug caps that you might
pick up on a walk in Bradgate Park, or deer droppings, scattered like runes, that
looked like black olives, and which, if you stared hard enough, would surely
reveal your future.

Weary of munitions' yards and inhaling oil, they, like so many, sought
recuperation in country parks in the shires even if it was in a hastily erected
outhouse building where cleanliness was not yet a priority.

Clouds pulled in opposite directions, trying to deliver two types of weather, in
the end, settling for an uneasy truce. Nonchalant young bucks sniffed at the
smells on the breeze, carrying the mottled maps of the past on their hides.

In the ladies' toilets, web-building had commenced. A worker had been
instructed to wash the walls down with hot soapy water but had been distracted
by a coach load of young women, just arrived from Birmingham.

How was he to know that the one that most caught his eye would write the
complaint— that, in the toilets, 'black spiders' webs were most frightful', and
that he would soon lose his job and would never know if the basis of her
complaint resulted from pure disgust because of a lapse on his part, or as a
result of the spiders' ineptitude at spinning.

JON WILKINS

Was born in Leicester, has entered his sixties and has a gorgeous wife Annie who is a retired Primary School teacher and two beautiful sons, David and Charlie. Jon loves to write poetry and crime. He has a Creative Writing MA from De Montfort University.

AN ATTEMPT AT EXHAUSTING A PLACE IN LEICESTER

I am sitting on the corner of Halford Street and Gallowtree Gate

> A pleasant place
> A quiet café
> Halford Street in front of me
> Gallowtree Gate to my right
> Prana sparkling as only it can
> Aromas of spice floating along the air
> Visit Leicester full of inquisitive tourists
> And interested parties

Slightly behind me

> Not quite in the centre of Leicester
> > Straight away shivers crease my body
> Gallowtree
> Where was the hangman's tree in times gone past?
> Who did they hang?
> And why?

I look out from my seat towards Granby Street straight ahead and then there is
Horsefair Street to my right
Market Place a bit further to my right
> The wonderful Nat West Bank building
On the corner of Horsefair Street and Granby Street
> Prana Cafe
A bit further on
All in my eye line
I know several buses will go past
Amongst them will be

> > 88 Bus

193

                                                          88A Bus
                                                           X6 Bus
                                                     48 Bus Arriva
                                                          X84 Bus
                                                           87 Bus
                                                  48 Bus Nuneaton

Most have different starting points
Most have different ending points
Some have the same routes
Strange that
                Saffron Lane
                Market Harborough
                Nuneaton
                Leicester University
                Bedworth
Arriva
Stagecoach
First Bus

                I can see the sky
                Blue and Grey
                Steel
                White puffs of cloud
                Birds
Pigeons
So many pigeons
                                        Café Nero
Strong Americano
Dash of milk
No cake
                                Perfect
                                        Well I would love cake

A couple enter the Nat West Bank
Hand in hand
A beggar in purple sits on a sleeping bag outside
Hoping and hoping

                                                              194

A man smokes in a reflective vest
    Obscene yellow
Two girl's hand in hand
Pink haired girl with boyfriend pass

                               X84 from Lutterworth

Man with blue Skeechers bag
Yellow dustbin lorry
Taxi
Man with disability trolley pushes by

                               20 Blackmore Drive

Girl eating cake
Daughter holds out hand
Hoping
Doesn't get any
Black baseball cap
Two women with pushchair

                               86 Eyres Monsell

Full to the brim
Blue car down Halford street
White van to Gallowtree gate

    Push chair
    Push chair
    Unrelated
Woman with black hair
Two Chinese girls
Students?
Look happy

                               88A from Saffron Lane

Empty
Where is everyone?
Chinese boy engrossed in phone
Girl with headphones
Black Toyota turns down Halford Street
                  Beggar gone
                  Sleeping bag remains
Blue Toyota down Halford street

Asian chap with walking stick
Lad in hoody
Non-threatening

Blue jacketed woman
Yellow west Indian coat
Beggar returns
Married couple in red to Gallowtree Gate
Black girl with headphones
White girl on smart phone
Red Volvo down Halford Street
Man with flat cap and walking stick
Finish coffee
Shiver as slightly cold and stretch legs
Stiffening up

88 via Freemans Park

Ginger haired woman
Blue jacketed man holding his glasses case
White Enterprise van
Beggar joined by female friend
Vigorous discussion starting
Couple waving over my head into the café
   Women with pushchair strolling down Gallowtree
   Gate
   Doesn't take eyes off phone
Somali men walk down Halford Street
Loud
White Jumper
Blue t shirt
Adidas hoody
Red bandana

Two Asian men
White haired woman
All to my right

48 from Nuneaton

Not many passengers

Green hoody
Black fiesta from Granby Street
Cream Toyota same direction
Man pushing bike
Nero employee wiping tables
Blue Audi
Man with red ruck sac
                    Pigeon
Wrestling with baguette
Beggar gone again
Sleeping bag remains
                              Asian couple
                              Hand in hand
                                        White couple
                                        Arguing

White BMW
White Mercedes
Halford Street backing up
Smell the car fumes
        Cough
Go inside to reorder coffee.
Somali woman in blue
                    Pigeons
                    So many pigeons
Red puffer jacket
Blue Suzuki
Beggars back
Alone
Large African family pass me from my left
TNT lorry from Granby Street
Beggars friend lights her a cigarette
She is dressed in purple
Bradgate Brook van
                                                  49 bus

Where does that go?

                                                  84 bus

Asian woman heavy bags

White Ford
Uber black taxi deposits Chinese couple

                                                    85 bus

Uber goes down Halford street
                Blue Vauxhall
                White Toyota
                Grey Peugeot
Gold and white spotted trouser girl
Red Renault drops off at Market Place
Young lad on a mobility scooter

                                        88 Eyres Monsell

Full
Taxi parks up to my right
Eurotaxi down Halford Street
Baseball cap man talking to himself
Lad in shorts and rucksack enters Gallowtree Gate

                        87 with a Birmingham University advert
Multicoloured coated white haired woman sits at table next to me
Starts to smoke
My coffee arrives
Thought they had forgotten me
                Baseball capped black lad in puffer jacket crosses road
                Walking towards Granby Street
                Shouting down smart phone
An internet van drives to my left

A big red BMW passes to my left
The woman driver seems to be too small
A woman in black but with colourful leggings walks past me to my left
Asian girl takes selfie
Blue tracksuit top guy makes for Horsefair Street
Im feeling a little chilled
Yellow bin van down Horsefair
Muslim woman in Red hijab

                                Girl with belly showing
                                She must be cold!

3 Somali girls

Shouting
Russian looking chap joins smoking woman
Beggars back
               Pigeons
               So many pigeons
Girl in grey hoody with slushy
Man with bags from market
Silver Merc with L plates

                                     48 South Wigston

Grey Citroen from Granby street
Black Vauxhall
Have I seen them already?
Two Muslim women
               Chinese girl in mask
               Friend playing Pokémon Go
Grey Renault
Man on phone
Girl strolling
Girl with rucksack
Woman pushing baby towards Gallowtree Gate
Black Mercedes
Red Suzuki
               Police car from Market Street
               First sight of a policeman today

                                     48 Nuneaton

Man on bike wearing Arriva uniform
Man in Leicester Tigers T shirt
Beggar joined by man
Another man joins them
Old Asian man leaves Bank
Followed by younger Asian man
               Another mobility scooter passes me by
               Its occupier is listening to the radio

A woman goes into the café
We smile a greeting
My coffee is drunk

I need to move
I order another coffee
I stand behind the woman
She takes a brie and cranberry wrap
     And a coffee
Must be lunch
This time
Red coated woman with large hand bag passes to my left
Blue coated woman with shopping bag enters Café
Limping Sikh
     Autistic woman with coffee cup passes
Glamorous woman in faux leather with large black sunglasses
No sun to show
Sky still blue
Woman in leggings goes into café
Beggars back to just two
     Muslim with Serious Bag
Young black lad listening to music
Big earphones

              88A
        48 from South Wigston
Empty
South American girl looks lost
Chinese man smoking and coughing
Black Nissan
2 yellow fluorescent vests
Black Nike Air jumper
Asian chap sipping Starbucks
Bowed old man
     Safety helmeted pair in dirty overalls walk towards Granby Street
Man in thick raincoat even though it's quite warm
Muslim woman pushing mobility frame

Huge pink pram down Gallowtree Gate
     Brave girl in pink t and leggings
Looks frozen
Pink headphones man goes towards Granby Street

All this pink all of a sudden!

49 City Centre

So that where it goes!
Black taxi from Granby Street

Girl in green top
Man in puffer top
Blue/white chinois leggings cyclist
Smiling Muslim man
Goth girl enters café
Taxi from Market Street
2 cyclists down Gallowtree Gate

Woman running

Crow pecking at something
White taxi
2 cyclists, have they returned?
Muslim in sandals
Crying baby in pushchair

Deliveroo cycling to my right
Pigeon leaves Halford Street
Cyclist walking with girl
Grey bearded Asian smoking to my left
Fluorescent jacket man checking phone
Woman with shopping and small child crossing road to Horsefair street
Man looking at travel brochure
Cyclist following boy down Horsefair street
Woman sits at end table
Lights cigarette
Opens novel
Can't see what she is reading

X6 Bus

Asian man on phone
Blue/Grey transit passes
Man pushes woman in wheelchair towards Market Place
Man striding down middle of road
Luckily pause in traffic!

201

Man passes to my right carrying impressive suitcase
      Woman on phone stands in middle of pavement
      Girl on phone passes her
      Old couple struggle to get by woman has a stick
      Woman on phone moves to side

Renault van reverses into Gallowtree gate
Couple hand in hand to my right
Asian boy very loud on phone using his hands a lot
Afro-Caribbean girl on phone
Asian couple walk down Halford Street, man leads
2 Somali girls shouting at each other, but not arguing
               48 Coventry bus

Packed
2 loud women
Followed by hipster in coat
Really hot now
      Pigeons
      So many pigeons

Tattooed leg man in cap to my right
2 men on phones pass each other
Cyclist goes down Granby Street
Woman leaves café
Arabic couple on phones
      3 hipsters now, leaving Nat West
Man with rucksack dodges man on bike
A couple passes to my left. White man black girl

Woman with gaily coloured scarf crosses road
White lads smoking and talking
Blue jacketed Asian man passes
Mini digger lurches across road towards Market Place Deliveroo lad on scooter
stops at corner
   Black ford passes him
Grey Citroen goes down Halford Street
      Deliveroo girl on bike stops by scooter
A woman with dyed blond hair pops into café

Jeans, hoody with pushchair and baby
    Another Deliveroo scooter arrives
Conference meeting?
Two women with pushchairs and phones cross to Horsefair Street
Silver Merc passes
       Deliveroo cyclist arrives travelling wrong way down road
       2 Deliveroo scooters leave
Oriental supermarket van drives down Halford Street

Navy Jaguar growls down Granby street
Taxi
Man passes with cigarette in his mouth
Black Audi

                                                84 bus

Somali pushing child in pushchair
Red Peugeot passes to my left
McKenzie hoody on girl
Asian family leave café
Middle-aged well-dressed couple walking up Market Place
Muslim couple walking to my right
       Couple leave table
       No more cigarette smoke
One of beggars on their way
Black VW
White Vauxhall
Black taxi
        Halford Street backing up again
     Man in grey pushing mobility frame
Boy drinking from water bottle
Older couple hand in hand
Another laden with shopping
All going down Halford Street
Cream Toyota
Camouflage shorts walks past beggar
Still talking

                                                88 bus

Huge West Indian man. Reverse baseball cap. Really long dreads

                                                        88A bus

Post Office van parks outside bank

                                                        20 bus

Not seen a 20 for a while
Now where does that go?
Post Office van now reversing towards Gallowtree Gate
            Grey taxi
Yellow council mini bus down Halford Street
Post Office van waiting for bollards to lower
Beggars chatting still
Grey Honda
            Woman with luggage going towards station I assume
Grey VW
Couple exit café each drinking coffee
                  PO van gets past bollards
                  VW now stuck in traffic
                  White van behind him
                  Grey mini
                  Fumes attacking me again

                                                        86 bus

Girl with luggage going down Granby Street
Wonder where she is off to
Beggars gone
Sleeping bag remains
Bald man with sunglasses and camouflage jacket
Woman with messy bun going down Gallowtree Gate
                  Blue Adidas top enters Horsefair street
Deliveroo down Granby Street
First of the day
White haired woman
Grey haired Muslim

                              Gang of Chinese students
                              All on phones
                              Pokémon Go?

Beggars belonging's unattended
Trust
Burgundy Peugeot SUV

White haired woman with trolley
Muslim girl in pink scarf
Silver Merc
Have I seen that before?
Black VW
    J777AKO
Asian woman with silver walking stick

                  Pigeons
                  So many pigeons
Brightly jacketed woman returns from down Granby Street
Oldish couple hand in hand
Magtec van down Horsefair Street
2 lads smoking not talking
Asian lady with shopping
Grey Merc
Black Nissan, loud music
        Asian woman actually talking to child in pushchair
        West Indian shopper, walking slowly
        Red dress down Gallowtree Gate
Cyclist
Silver BMW
Man in shorts
Brave!

                       49 bus

Beggars back
Couple drinking coffee smoking piercings
Family talking on corner to my right
Black lad, black cap, on phone

                       84 bus

Shetland jumper on phone
Grey BMW
2 out 2 in at Nat West
Man smoking at next table
Truckline van passes

                 48 from Nuneaton

Older couple arm in arm

                       83 bus

Destination?
Crowded
Girl with phone, not talking, listening
Beggar still there
Mobility scooter passes me

                As do 3 young lads
                Chatting
                Loudly

Asian couple
Group of 8 students

                                85 bus

Autistic woman returns

                                85 bus

Man talking to son
Man with white stick going down Gallowtree Gate
Man on phone shouting
Walking from Market Street
To my right
Sun coming out and quite warm now
Loud African man passes
Shouting to friend at his side

                                88 bus

Cyclist from Granby Street
Uber Eats
Man starting argument behind me
Grey BMW from Granby Street
Woman in pink top
Today's favourite colour?

                Silver Honda blasts horn at woman
                She shouts back
                Gives driver finger

                                88 bus

2 Muslim women
Man pushing woman in wheelchair
Man with Sainsburys shopping bag
White Merc drives into Market Place
Woman with pushchair sits by my side

Family arrives at café
Man
Woman
Small boy
Girl in pushchair
                                                    Noise
Man disappears into café
Boy sits and plays with playmobile figure
Girl is asleep
I ask them to watch my things
I go for another coffee
Hear woman shouting from Gallowtree Gate
I return
Neighbour asks what I'm writing
                    I try to explain
A white 4x4 drives to my right
A red Mini exits Granby Street
Two cyclists ride down the pavement
Another mobility scooter passes
(the same one?)
Blue Silver Honda SUV passes
Man with dog and luggage enters Gallowtree Gate

Beggar woman greets shouting woman
Girl in red puffer jacket on phone
Man with newspaper
2 girls talking one has JD bag
Muslim man passes to my left and crosses road
                                                    X6 bus
Quite full
But it has come a long way
Asian chap in black baseball cap
Woman with two children in her pushchair
Woman in pink puffer jacket
I rest my case!
                    Beggar gone

Vanished
Sleeping bag gone
Disappeared
Grandma, Dad and daughter pass
Cyclist
Road sweeper drives down Market Place
Bald headed body builder ambles by
A new beggar is going down the café tables
Asking for 10p
Doesn't ask me
White van down Halford Street

87 bus
88A bus

Woman on phone
Man in flat cap
Passing Boy asks for a rizla from a café client
He takes two
Woman in Nike top
Couple girl in Ted Baker
Man next to me talking to neighbour about weight gain
Man now looking for tobacco, not sure if same one
Woman in suit
High powered!
Cyclist
Deliveroo again
Blind man with stick

48 from Coventry

Blows horn at pedestrians crossing in front of him
Couple pass
Woman in hijab
White ford
Man pushing pram
Followed by woman in hijab
Man in blue T shirt

Mother and daughter
Chatting
Loudly

Aggressively
Taxi with orange stripe
Man in smart coat
Couple chatting smiling
Girl on phone
Couple walking, both on phones
Grey Toyota passes to my left
White van follows
White Vauxhall

84 bus

Just misses a pink haired girl who runs last few steps
Traffic snarling again
Chinese couple
Older couple

48 South Wigston

Yellow hatted man
Black Merc parks on Market Street
Illegally
Black Ford SUV blast horn at him

Pink haired woman wandering
Wondering?

Diet conversation continuing
Stop drinking seems to be the message
Beggar back
As is sleeping bag
Silver Toyota passes

Asian women chatting
Sikh man in yellow turban
Woman in Blue 60s mod cap

Asian couple, one bald
Purple VW
Girl with "Fight Animal Testing" bag
Older couple pass, then they split up walk in different directions

Black Merc now flashing warning lights
Deliveroo down Horsefair Street
Cyclist down Gallowtree Gate

Cyclist towards Market Place
Yellow bin lorry into Market Place

                                                    Pigeons
                                              So many pigeons

White Enviropest van
Woman on bike passes me by
Pipe Centre lorry on Granby Street
White Uber taxi

                                                    88 bus

Older couple in pink and grey puffer jackets
Young Asian girl walks towards Gallowtree Gate
Man with vape
First vape of the day
Road sweeper slowly cleans the gutters of Granby Street
Boy with subway
Silver VW
                2 Asian chaps in conversation
Painter in spattered dungarees passes down Horsefair Street
Asian couple chatting
I get up and stretch to the sky
Sun shining
I pack away my notebook
                        My pens
                  Finish my cold coffee
                          Make my way home